Set Adrift

Immortal Isle Series

DS Kenn

Dedication

This book is dedicated to Shannon and to Joe. The two of you inspire me in little ways and big ways and heart stopping ways, every single day. I have never once doubted that you would be there to catch me if I stumbled, even when I deserved to fall on my face.

Between the two of you, I have learned courage and independence and strength. You've shown me what loyalty, humility, empathy, and true caring can do. You've supported me in every crazy idea I have ever had; your belief in me is both humbling and terrifying. You've both held me when I've faltered and when I've broken, and never once have you made me feel like less because of it. You've put up with my yelling, my temper, my moods, and my silences.

Joe, I have never seen anyone who is as steadfast as you. Through all the frustrations and the setbacks, you keep moving forward, and you do it with patience and kindness. I watch you with those who are weaker, those who look to you for care and love. They know that they are safe and that they will never be forgotten and will never be alone. To me, that is the measure of a human being.

Shannon, you are a part of my soul. You are what keeps me going and what keeps me trying over and over again to become a better person, to be the parent that you deserve. When I think of you, of our life together and watching you grow up, the thing that sticks out the most is the laughter. I hope that it's that way for you as well. You have left me speechless on many occasions and breathless on a few. I watch you walk into the world and grab life with both hands and I want to drag you back, but I don't, because I am too busy applauding the person you are.

Thank you, both. For putting up with me. For putting up with the writing, the group, the computer, and the book. I hope someday you read these stories and know that you are in each and every one of them, as you are in each and every part of my life. I love you.

Acknowledgments

This list will be long and heartfelt, and writing it has me filled with both anxiety and trepidation. Any and all who know me know that my memory is a beyond terrible. So if I have forgotten to list you here, know that I have ever been grateful to you and will offer up a sincere apology in advance.

My parents, Tom and Linda, deserve a tremendous thank you for their unflagging belief in me. They taught me how to work hard and go after what I want, and anything I've accomplished has been with the thought of making them proud.

My sister, Debbie, has always been there to help through this parenting minefield. I would never have made it through college if it weren't for her selflessly picking my daughter up every day. My kiddo spent so much time there she called her Uncle Mark "Daddy," which earned us some odd looks, but that's okay. We like to make people think. I remember Shannon walking in to their house and asking, "What's for dinner, Daddy?" and he didn't blink an eye, just answered her, and she would head off to play with her cousins, Tia and Tamarah. My family made it possible for me to chase after dreams and know that my child was well cared for and loved.

My brother David was always the voice of reason, and I knew that if I needed to talk, he was the one to call. He had a way of putting things in perspective and getting me to calm down and think. He is the person I connect with most in the world, and I would be lost completely if I didn't have him as an anchor.

I am also thankful for my brother Danny, who has recently become part of my life once again, and whose wit and humor I have missed these last few years.

I dedicated this book to Joe and Shannon, but they also need to be acknowledged here with the rest of my family, all of them have put up with me writing when I should have been interacting. They have selflessly picked up my slack and encouraged me, supported me, and believed in me. My family truly is incredible.

I have some amazing friends to thank as well. Lucia Ludewig. I type her name and then just pause and stare at all the space that is left on the page and wonder if it is going to be enough. I have never had a friend as loyal as she, ever. I doubt anyone has. We met through random chance in an odd corner of the Internet, and we have been friends ever since. She has propped me up, let me vent, and given me moral support.

Janet Romano is another incredible friend I have met on this insane path. She helped me get DnD (our writing group) off the ground and running, and aside from being an awesome writing partner, she helped translate when my crazy got in the way.

Speaking of the group... to all the amazing writers (both past and present) to grace DnD with their talent, I want to thank them from the bottom of my heart. They shared their creativity, their skill, and their heart with me and the readers and the other writers. That place was all that it was, because of them. A special shout out to Sue Allen Milkovich, who was DnD's biggest champion and cheerleader from the very first day. Thank you to all the incredibly loyal and supportive readers that took the time to care about the characters and the world we created.

Thank you, also, to the following people... Their friendship and support have meant so much to both the group and to me personally.

Kallypso Masters, a huge thank you for taking the time to sit with a reader in NOLA, at an AAD convention where I am sure she was already run ragged. She allowed me to ask questions, and her candor and advice were invaluable. Even now, years later, she continues to mentor and give of herself. I am so thankful for all her recommendations and for taking me seriously, I know it would have been easy not to.

Damon Suede, I'm grateful he took the time to chat with me at AAD and on Facebook, and for his invaluable advice on marketing, websites, and the world of publishing. Also, many thanks to him for wearing a kilt now and then, and for posting the photos on FB.

JT Cheyanne, VL Moon, Inês Madanelo, Rissa Angelo, Anna Miller, Chantel Krueger-Wiegmann, Linda Von H, Dana Richey, Shelly McCreery, and Anne Beate Sæthre. All have meant different things to me over the years. One thing I could always count on was support, caring, laughter, and friendship. And from some of them, I got the added bonus of foreign language porn.

Eva, who was my writing partner for years. I will always have mad love for her. I am so proud of all she's accomplished.

I had some great beta readers. Beth Allen, Jackie Primo, Brandy Page, Mandi Konesni, Melanie Casillas, Kayla Swann, and Lisa Burris. Lisa is also an amazing writing partner; her fearlessness helped me learn and grow and push past comfort zones.

Jacy Mackin, who spent time helping me, not just as an editor but in navigating this brutally complicated and terrifying landscape. Also, many thanks for not strangling me when it turned out that Mac pages doesn't really play nicely with the editing side of Word.

Kari Ayasha at Cover to Cover designs… She did a beautiful job on the cover, and I am thankful for the way she brought my vision for it to life.

Meredith Bowery for her awesome editing. I know that my abuse of "its and it's" drove her a bit batty.

Thank you to Karen Candido, for taking time out of her day to drive in to Boston and meet someone new and then taking us to Maine the next day. She did that for a stranger, just so I could take pictures of lighthouses and get attacked by seagulls. It was a great day.

Thank you also to Ryan Collins, who owns the website where I found the perfect lighthouse photo. It had to be a Provincetown lighthouse, and his website, www.myfishing-capecod.com had the perfect picture of one. I had to have it. So I messaged him, and he got me in touch with the incredibly talented photographer, Michael Morin. These two were gracious enough to send me the file and allow me to use it, and that just blew me away. You don't find many people that kind nowadays, especially not to strangers or writers just starting out.

I loved writing in school, of course. It was always my favorite thing. And then life got in the way. An employee at Borders, Jenn, introduced me to a book series that I fell in love with, and in a roundabout way, that got me writing once more. Over the years, I have written in many different groups on Facebook. Thank you, to all those various groups and writers. What I remember most from that time is laughter, friendship, and some truly amazing talent. Many people have helped, inspired, and offered advice, and not all of them are listed here. It would be impossible to even try. Thank you for the lessons learned, and for the chance to grow.

Brand Acknowledgment

Blanton's Bourbon ® by Blanton's Distilling Co®

Devil's Cut® by Jim Beam®

Sleep Number®

Tempur-Pedic®

Camaro ZL1 by Chevrolet®

Prologue

DAYLIGHT HAD BROKEN. For the first time in decades, Terric Blythe stood before the ocean as the sun rose. His back grazed the lighthouse as he inhaled deeply of the beach air. The move from New York to Provincetown, Massachusetts, had mainly been for Jordyn Kinsley, the woman he shared his life with.

In New York, they isolated themselves out of necessity. He was a hybrid demon and wolf shifter; she a vampire. Keeping their nature secret permitted Jordy to hide out, avoid facing life by only doing the bare minimum to endure. She survived, but she never lived. Though Terric didn't blame her and certainly sympathized with her, he refused to allow her to castigate herself forever as she withdrew until, eventually, she disappeared completely. He had enabled her long enough.

Terric had heard of a place where they could live among others of their kind, in a far more open manner. They could move about as they chose, interacting with other paranormals or with humans if they wanted. He had broached the topic with her slowly, easing her into the idea. At first, she had simply nodded, as if she humored him. Perhaps she thought he would never actually do it.

Nothing bound them to New York, however. Their only ties were to each other. Despite the few relationships he had indulged in over the years, he had never become attached to any of the women. Jordyn was the first paranormal to ever find residence in his heart. Prior to Jordyn, he had loved a human woman, Michelle, in his way. The knowledge that the affair could only be temporary was all that allowed him to feel for her. If they were to spend the entirety of her lifespan together, it still would register as no more than a moment on the long timeline of his life. They had barely managed to stay together two years; when she had discovered his true nature, she had drawn the relationship to an abrupt halt.

Still, he never regretted showing her what he was, at the time or years later, when examining the relationship and decisions made. Michelle had recognized him for the monster he was, and she fled back to her family and the oppressive confines of their protection. And Terric bid her well as he watched her go. He had known then her choice was for the best, for both of them. Demons exist at the whim of a sadistic master, and having her in his life provided far more fuel to be used against him than made him comfortable. Humans were much too delicate.

The sky grew lighter, the burning colors reflected in his brown eyes. His thoughts turned once more to their new home of Provincetown, where paranormal beings were respected, revered, and cared about by the human population. The arrangement was odd, but somehow it worked. The monsters lived peacefully among the locals, each looking out for the other. The paranormal predators took their hunting elsewhere, rarely harming any of their fragile human neighbors. As always, exceptions to the norm could be found, but they were dealt with swiftly and harshly.

The humans called the assorted beings among them "otherworlders." They enjoyed the fact that they secretly laid claim to something no other area could: Friendship, protection, and actual knowledge of beings that most people would consider myth, or nightmare. These humans lived and worked among them and had for well over a century. At first, fear and skepticism ran rampant, but the monsters were as drawn to the humans as the humans were to them. And Terric knew firsthand most paranormal beings grew weary; the idea of being able to settle down and live in an area that didn't hunt or expose them had its merits. The humans tended to provide a welcome distraction from a life that lasted centuries with little to break up the monotony.

When Terric had heard that a club in Provincetown was hiring, he dug beneath the surface to determine if it was the job for him. The owners, Vickie and Lucas, were relatively new to the area but knew their business well. Ascendance was a front for Trespass Trades, which supplied otherworlder clientele with pretty much anything they wanted to get their hands on. From munitions to paranormal pornography, everything had a price... Not that Terric cared, as long as everyone involved were consenting adults.

Terric heard the subtle difference as the tide changed. Eventually, it would go out completely, and that low tide would mean death for any living thing unable to react and move with the direction the currents demanded. Death would be preceded by long, agonizing suffering while it lay there and waited for the pain to pass and oblivion to take over. Most beings craved life, fought to sustain and enrich it, and attempted to give it sense and meaning. A starfish would dry out eventually, but not until it tried desperately to sink beneath sand that had hardened too much to yield and give it necessary shelter. Small organisms created their own worlds inside the scattered seashells. These small universes would later be gathered by humans walking the beach and looking for souvenirs. The shells would inevitably be laid on the back steps leading up to a rented beach house until they dried out. The smell of decay would be washed away with bleach until nothing except the superficial beauty of the shell remained.

He and Jordyn, at their most basic level, were incomplete, missing some essential element that would tell them who they were. As paranormal creatures, they were closer to animal than to human in many aspects, more primal and less cerebral. Theirs was an intelligence born more of instinct than of scholarly pursuits. That he was half-demon made it more difficult for Terric to reconcile who and what he was. He had often wondered if he possessed a soul, but he knew animals had one, so that meant he did as well, the soul of the wolf. Because of this, he endured a harsher, crueler truth; the suffering he inflicted on others, he felt as well. Luckily, the ability to read people helped him eliminate collateral damage in delivering undeserved punishment. Still, he did not take souls or inflict harm lightly, and never without cost to himself in the process.

Terric's temper was legendary, and his fury rose each time he thought of what had been done to Jordyn. Evil driven by madness had torn through her life, nearly destroying her. She had ignored her own powerful intuition and the warnings of others out of a misguided sense of love, blinding her to the man's insanity. Madness in a paranormal being was nearly always fatal to all within striking distance. Jordyn had suffered greatly at the hands of the man who had sworn to cherish her, love her, and protect her. The monster that had taken so much from her had made a mockery of every promise he had made and, in the cruelest act of all, had left her alive to bear constant witness to an unrelenting, paralyzing pain. She could try to shelter herself, but she couldn't escape the images. She heard his vicious taunts in the middle of the night and always felt the cage closing in on her, making it nearly impossible to draw in a full breath. These nightmares had woken Terric, drawn them into her mind to see what she was reliving.

Everyone that she had loved was taken from her, and her sense of inadequacy was cemented when her mate had wrenched her child, their child, screaming, from her and left Jordyn lying there, broken and helpless, begging, while he casually threw his son's suddenly lifeless body down next to those of her parents. He had told her she was worthless, that he had taken those lives as a payment for her sins. She had stared at him, her mind unable to comprehend the madness even while her heart shattered. Jordyn thought wildly of her brother, wanting him to come and save her, to undo all that had transpired. Her brother had implored her for years to leave her mate and, when that hadn't worked, had raged and threatened. Still, she hadn't listened, and her mistake had cost her loved ones far too high a price. Terric's hands shook as he remembered the scene, one he had been horrified to witness from her perspective after the fact. He wanted nothing more than to go back to that moment, see the monster standing over her, and destroy it.

Finding Jordyn had been a fluke. Such a stench surrounded the home that Terric had been drawn there and had been shocked to find out that the premises had been devoid of all inhabitants save Jordy for nearly a year. Her brother had shown up while the carnage was still fresh and, upon taking in the scene, had set off after the mate, leaving Jordyn alone. She was nearly dead when Terric found her, and she begged to be freed from the suffering.

Terric had never found what gave his life meaning, and Jordyn had been robbed of what made her life worthwhile. He was able to give her a part of himself he hadn't known existed. He couldn't change the trajectory of her life before he met her, but he could give her the security and peace of mind to try to find what would make her whole once again. She wouldn't be who she was before, but he saw glimpses of who she could become. His Jordyn was a fighter. She was far too cautious, and she tended to overcompensate for past mistakes. Jordy now tried to examine options from every possible angle, but when she made up her mind to do something, she put her entire heart into it, and she became a force in her own right.

The move to Provincetown was one more step in the process, in bringing Jordyn back to who she was before. And unintentionally, the move would bring Terric one step closer to finding out who he could become as well.

Chapter One

THE CLUB, ASCENDANCE, was packed. Terric parked his truck around the side, beneath the stairs leading to the emergency exit. For a while, no one came down. He just watched the patrons as they arrived, left their vehicles with the valet, and headed for the front door. After some time, a silver Mercedes pulled up, its windows tinted beyond legal. The driver parked in a reserved spot underneath a light. The male walked around and opened the passenger door. Lucas Stone and Victoria, aka Vickie, Kingston.

Their hands reached for each other out of long habit as the sleek couple headed toward the stairs. Terric watched them closely, knowing he was being observed at that moment as well. The club owner and her mate turned toward him in unison, but made no move to approach. The male moved the female closer to him in a classically protective gesture as they started up the stairs, his body angled so that he was always between her and any potential threat.

Finally, satisfied he had seen enough, Terric exited the truck and ambled up to the front door. He gave the bouncer his name, and after a moment, a guy in a well-tailored suit came to greet him. Knowledge flickered in the human's eyes as he quickly assessed the being before him; he knew that most of the other people in the crowd were not like him, and Terric clearly had set off some instinctive warning. The man led Terric through the crowd and into a quieter section of the club, asking him to wait a moment before quietly disappearing back into the throng of dancing bodies.

When the couple from outside came out, they led Terric to a table near the back. It gave a good view of the action in the club, but was still relatively private. Though the VIP section was full, the patrons there appeared to be quieter and more reserved than the general population sweating and eye-fucking each other out on the dance floor or in the main bar area.

The three of them sat quietly, appraising, quietly assessing, and—in the case of Lucas and Terric—reading each other. Their demonic nature allowed them to see far more than most, even other supernatural beings, would pick up on. They were both hybrids, both only half demon. Still, that half gave them the ability to shield, to block others from reading them. Shielding from each other was far more difficult, granted; it was more obvious and taxed them more, mentally.

Eventually, Lucas spoke. His voice was measured, neutral. "I heard about you some, Blythe. A demon shifter, you've been in the security business in some form or another for over a century. You're insanely private. There's rumor of a hot blonde you like to play with, but not mated or, if it's the wolf that is doing it, bonded. You have few friends, you seem to hate being a demon, and you don't play all that well with others. So tell me. Why do I want to hire you?"

Terric sat back in his chair, glancing at the waitress as she hesitated uncertainly at their table. He nodded at her, asked for a water, and then continued as she wandered off. "You want someone you can trust to run both of your businesses while you see to your other interests. I've been in security for a long time, in just about every capacity. I'm honest, I don't touch what isn't mine, and I don't fuck around with people. I take my responsibilities seriously."

The heavy silence lay between them as he weighed his next words. Terric uncapped and drank deeply from the bottle of water that had been quietly set in front of him before he continued. "Provincetown has nothing else like what you offer, and the atmosphere here is a good one for us and others like us. There is a large otherworld population here. Every species and being you can think of is represented in this area, the only area in the world like it." Terric recapped the water bottle and set it down, leaning back with his arm slung across the seat back next to him. His eyes were a deep russet brown, appearing nearly black in certain lighting. They took in every detail of his surroundings, cataloguing, memorizing, filing the information away.

"You need someone to help with security and day to day operations, plus the other matters that arise in dealing with your Trespass clientele. We have mutual... acquaintances in the other realm that can provide any references you may need. I think you'll find that I am more than capable of handling whatever comes my way." Terric's face grew closed off. "However, my personal life is my own. You heard correctly, I value my privacy above all else."

Lucas leaned forward, intelligence sparking in his eyes. He let his gaze roam over Terric, trying to pick beneath the layer that was buried just out of his reach. He held silent for several beats, waiting for the other male to squirm or offer up more information. Nothing. *Fucking demons.* Lucas picked up the glass of Blanton's the waitress had automatically brought him, swirling the high-end bourbon and letting the silence grow. Finally, a humorless smile crossed his face. "So, Terric, I also heard you aren't afraid to die. That, in fact, at times you court it. I am great with having an employee willing to give his life for Vickie's. Absolutely. However, I am not interested in someone with a death wish walking around our house endangering people because safety is for losers, you know? Which is it? Lack of fear or the actual desire for death, or whatever the equivalent is for beings such as us? Let's be honest, T. May I call you that? I believe that's how your friends refer to you?"

Terric's expression didn't change, but he inclined his head in a gesture of assent as he leaned forward and picked up his water once again. His eyes met Lucas', and his voice was quiet, his answer simple. "I don't endanger others, ever, if I can help it. I guess the honest answer is both. I don't fear death, and at times, I desire it. Believe me, when it happens, it won't be here, and it won't involve innocent lives. Tomorrow soon enough for me to start?" The two exchanged glances, something imperceptible passing between them before Lucas nodded.

Vickie smiled and asked Terric if he needed lodging. Terms and payment were discussed and agreed upon, and they all stood. No handshake was exchanged between the males. Neither would have felt comfortable having physical contact with another demon, especially one that was still unfamiliar to them. Vickie rose on her tiptoes and kissed

Terric's cheek lightly, her expression welcoming. Terric awkwardly hugged her and watched Lucas take her hand and draw her subtly closer to his body.

His new employer hadn't appeared to enjoy his female touching Terric, but she hadn't seemed all that concerned about his displeasure. She knew how to handle her mate. Terric watched with interest as she flashed a mischievous grin and then turned her gaze to Lucas, a playfully innocent expression on her face. Lucas murmured something quietly to her, Terric's keen ears clearly hearing every word of the low warning. He wasn't concerned that the demon would harm Vickie, however. Quite the opposite, she seemed intent on seeing how far she could push before Lucas made good on his promise. Terric turned his attention elsewhere, pretending not to be aware of the arousal that shot through Vickie as Lucas reminded her to behave. Finally, Lucas leaned down and put his mouth at Vickie's ear, his tongue sliding along soft flesh as he chuckled softly and whispered, "We're leaving, Vixen. Say goodnight." Vickie stammered out a hasty goodbye, not making eye contact with Terric as Lucas firmly held her arm and escorted her to the door.

Terric sat back down for a couple hours to watch how the place ran. He would learn far more watching for a brief time while still anonymous than he would in a week once they knew who he was. He selected a couple employees that would be removed at the start of his first shift. They had an agenda of their own and were selling their own product to the customers. No one who would do business on the side knew shit about loyalty, and therefore, they were a liability.

Before he left, T had memorized five faces that were going to be gone, leaving a few openings in the bar staff and among the bouncers. He was unconcerned. He did both jobs well enough, and honest people seeking work were always in abundance.

HE ROSE AND took a walk around the club to see what security issues might exist in the layout. It wasn't bad; these two knew what they were doing. That made his job even more enjoyable. As he walked out, he nodded to some of the staff, stopping for a moment to introduce himself to the bouncer at the door. He had no need to hide any longer, far better to let the staff speculate about what he saw and what he was like. The ones that were going to panic and flee could do so now, before he officially started and ended up being in the position of hunting them down if they stole on their way out. He was giving them a head start, a chance to remove themselves before he could take their actions personally.

As he walked across the parking lot, he noted some deals going on outside the club, patrons selling to each other. That would stop as well. It made the classiest of places look like shit and prompted nightly visits from cops, which tended to keep decent customers away.

Remaining on good terms with the local cops would be even more essential here. The area had two police departments that shared a symbiotic relationship. An unusual one that seemingly worked very well. The arrangement was comprised of the regular police force, for the human population and a paranormal one for the otherworlders. Each policed his own, and the only time the two overlapped was when a crime was committed by one populace upon the other. If a supernatural being committed a heinous enough crime on a human, the human police would weigh in on the punishment and perhaps be there to see it drawn out. If the opposite were true, same rules applied. The paranormal police tended to exact the punishment on their own, as the humans simply didn't have the strength. In the case of a truly horrific crime, the punishment recommended by the side of the victim would be upheld. However, it really hadn't been an issue in Provincetown. The populace there lived well side-by-side; each group enjoyed what they received from the relationship.

Terric had done his research thoroughly before moving Jordy and himself down to the tip of Cape Cod from New York. She deserved happiness, and if he couldn't give her that, at the very least peace. She already loved being in this place. She had breathed easier since the moment they had arrived, and her smile came more readily now that they were settling in than it had in all the time he had known her. Terric glanced at his watch and stood to go home and make sure she knew that they were staying. He had told her they were, but until she was at ease that he had work he could enjoy here, she wouldn't believe him.

The parking lot of the apartment building was nearly empty. Only a few tenants lived there year round. Late at night, most people would be asleep. He parked next to his neighbor's little sedan and looked around, testing the darkness for movement that might be out of place. The precaution was merely habit; he wasn't expecting anything. The purpose of coming here had been to live in a place they could relax and be themselves, whenever they figured out who that was. He grabbed the flowers he had picked up for her; white roses with some small pink flowers mixed in, and stepped down from the truck. He made sure his truck was locked then headed to the stairs. He punched in the security code and silently slipped in rather than flashing into their home. They always strove for relative normalcy and anonymity when in possible view of humans.

Jordy was dozing on the couch, resting easy for once. T made little noise as he strode past her into the kitchen to find a vase for the flowers. He arranged them as best he could; he basically just cut them out of the wrapper, removed the stems, and set them in some water. He left a small light on over the stove and headed in to the shower.

Terric stood there under the spray for a while, letting the heat relax his muscles. His eyes were closed, palms laying flat against the wall, his back to the door when it opened. He felt cool air snake in to replace the heat his body had been absorbing and sensed Jordyn's presence as she wordlessly observed him. He didn't say anything, didn't move. She needed to do this sometimes, needed to adjust to his nearness before she could settle. When he had given her what he considered adequate time, he took one hand off the wall and held it out to her, beckoning her to join him. He turned his head slightly, so she could see his eyes. That also helped calm her. When they were red, she, like everyone else, stayed far away.

Her face was a mask of determination as she dropped her robe, revealing her flawless body with lush curves and a tiny waist. She entered and stood just inside the shower, hands clasped behind her back, the steam causing her long hair to curl slightly around her stunning face. Her skin was a golden color uniquely gifted to some natural blondes. Not a single blemish or imperfection dared to mar her complexion. Jordyn was what many would consider the gold standard for beauty. Nature's cruel joke: she craved anonymity and solitude, yet people were drawn to her constantly, all people, everywhere. Children especially, perhaps because she looked like a princess from a fairy tale. Unfortunately, she was as damaged on the inside as she was beautiful on the outside.

As Jordyn stood before him, waiting, Terric sighed inwardly and forced himself to push such thoughts from his mind. She didn't need sympathy or coddling. She came to him because he was able to see past her sadness and her comely features to what was inside her and give her what she needed. She needed love, and she needed physical contact, but only under a stringent set of circumstances. He was able to be firm with her, strict even, and still shower her with affection and the right kind of tenderness at the right moments.

Without warning, he wrapped his fingers around her forearm, spinning her face first into the wall. His movements were quick, not giving her time to panic at the contact as his body trapped hers against the wall. She gasped once as he nudged her legs farther apart with his knee, one hand between her shoulder blades and one hand on her hip, forcing her to bend over as he entered her in one smooth thrust. She was wet, her heat immediately surrounding him, and he closed his eyes to savor the way her body welcomed him.

Jordyn was having a good day then, hadn't waited too long to come to him. He released her hip, reached around, and began to part her folds, stroking her. He spoke to her finally. "Good girl, very good. I like when you pay attention to your body, Jordyn, when you pay attention and take care of yourself before we have to spend time in the other room to get here. Isn't this better, baby, just pleasure, no pain?"

She moaned at his voice in her ear, but her fast, silent nod said she hadn't come to him quite soon enough. He dropped his hand from her core, once more gripping her hip, roughly this time. He bent her over farther, withdrew from her pussy, and parted her ass cheeks. She became perfectly still, and he leaned down to the shelf, grabbed a bottle of lubricant, and poured some on his hand. Slowly, he massaged it into her, starting with the pert ass cheeks and working his way to the crease of her ass. His silence would unnerve her, but he didn't speak or offer any words that would calm her.

She shifted impatiently. He gave a sharp smack, leaving a red mark that he bent over and soothed with kisses, letting his tongue run up the cleft of her ass to the base of her spine. Finally, he began working a finger inside her ass, her body tightening before she forced herself to relax and allow him in. He added a second and a third finger, his other hand leaving her ass cheek momentarily to stroke her flank, the only warning she received before he removed his fingers and replaced them with his cock, entering her fully and stopping, allowing her to adjust to his size and relax her body once more. He began thrusting inside her, his hand in her hair, dragging her head back. His other hand slid up her flat belly, palming her breast before moving to her nipple and squeezing, using fingers in lieu of a clothespin and clamping down hard on the tiny nub.

The blond locks of hair were tangled around his hand, and he angled her head so he could see her face, her eyes, and he watched her carefully while his mouth sought the soft flesh of her neck, his lip pulled back to reveal a sharp canine. He didn't need her blood, but he would spill it and find enjoyment in the act and her taste. He sliced into her flesh, knowing that his canines weren't like her fangs, made for feeding from others. Still, they did the job, in more ways than

one. Jordyn was a vampire, and she was biologically pro-
grammed to want to feed a mate. The additional pain simply
brought her where she needed to be more quickly.

The first drops hit his tongue, and he felt his eyes start to
change as the demon part of his nature grew more aroused.
She let out a half sob, and he shifted his head slightly, gripping
her more firmly. When tears began to flow down her cheeks
and her lips parted as her breathing quickened, he knew she
had come back to him. The pain, even mingled with pleasure,
was enough for her to allow for him to be gentle with her
now. She would be able to accept his touch and the pleasure
he wanted to give her.

Terric released the hold his mouth had on her flesh. He
buried himself deep inside her ass for a moment longer,
fighting back his orgasm, before withdrawing from her body.
He turned her around to face him, picking her up and holding
her under the spray so the water fell over both of their bodies
and warmed them once more. He paused their lovemaking,
taking time to attend to her, making sure she was going to stay
with him. He picked up the washcloth, soaking it in hot water,
and then grabbed the soap. The scent was one he always
associated with Jordyn, a mixture of vanilla with a tropical
note. Terric began washing her, his eyes steady on hers while
he moved the cloth over her slippery body. He dipped it low,
moving between her legs, and she moaned lightly. Her lids
lowered as she raked her gaze over his body.

Jordyn took the cloth from him, rewetting and lathering it
again. She started first at his chest; her hand followed the
cloth as she let her fingers play over his skin, admiring the feel
of the hard muscles under her palm. She smiled softly,
enjoying the chance to look her fill and tend to him for a

change. Jordyn washed Terric, taking advantage of the opportunity to touch every inch of the man before her. She intended to heighten his arousal, but her own wouldn't be ignored any longer, and she set aside the soap, moving closer to him once more.

Terric opened his eyes and noted her expression. His Jordy needed. He moved them under the spray once more, rinsing them both thoroughly, and then he lifted her up, holding her against his body. He kissed her deeply, his eyes dark with arousal.

Jordyn wrapped her legs around his waist, her eyes now focused on his, present in the moment as he impaled her, her slick core gripping him tightly. He pinned her against the wall, the long muscles in his thighs flexing as he stroked inside her over and over again until her inner walls began to spasm with her release, milking the orgasm from him, a shout leaving his body as he climaxed. When her breathing had returned to normal and her orgasm had subsided, he withdrew from her and moved her under the spray to wash her.

Terric kissed her, delighting in the way she finally kissed him back fully, released from whatever demons held her immobile and unresponsive until he used pain to spring her from their grasp. He turned off the spray, stepped out, and grabbed a towel. He slung it around his waist before getting one for her and wrapping her in it, helping her from the shower and drying her off.

Terric would now be able to pet her and give her affection. He kissed a trail across her shoulder, his hands moving the towel lightly over her body. She stared at him, and he wondered what she saw. He used to frighten her, and he knew that was what had drawn her to him. She had thought he would be the monster he appeared to be, and she had been hoping he would kill her. He was not a classically handsome male. He was six feet three inches tall, his body muscular but lean. The demon in him was always apparent, just beneath the surface. He didn't seem different in a way that could be pointed to or quantified, but other people observing him instinctively sensed the danger there, a hint of barely restrained evil perhaps.

His father had been a demon, in every sense of the word, and had not resembled a human all that much. Terric's mother, on the other hand, had been a breathtakingly beautiful wolf shifter. His oddly colored brown eyes came from her, rich and deep wolf's eyes. That was the one feature that saved him, that let people know he did, in fact, have a soul, even though he questioned that himself quite often. His hair was a dark brown. Most of the time he kept it shaved close to his head, but when he did allow it to grow, he usually left it in the rumpled, unkempt style that came natural to him but others spent an hour and an army of products on.

Terric lifted Jordyn's slight form easily, despite her only being a couple inches shorter than him. As a vampire, she possessed the physical strength inherent in her species, which was undoubtedly why she had been unable to kill herself despite years of trying. He laid her down in their bed. They didn't share it every night, at most a few nights a week. He never left her alone for the night after they had made love.

The goal with every encounter they had was always to get her to a place she could accept touch and eye contact. To keep her engaged and present in the moment. Whether they spent hours bringing her pain until she broke and then accepted physical contact or they were able to just make love and keep her level, the idea was to keep her functioning and prevent her retreating to that place where no one could reach her.

Terric finished drying off and pulled on a pair of boxer briefs, lying down next to her. She curled on her side, facing him, her hand reaching up and stroking his cheek. She was not tentative or hesitant to touch him, a good sign. He grabbed her hand, bringing it to his mouth and kissing her palm. She sighed, her eyes closing for a moment before she spoke. Her voice was soft, as pleasing to the ear as her face was to the eye. "Thank you, Terric. I was okay, really okay, and then I started to slip away... I know you said to call you, but I've been holding up so well, have felt so normal. I'm so much closer to being well..." Her voice trailed off. Nothing she could say hadn't been said already.

Terric knew her, everything about her. She stared at him, often when he wasn't aware. He was beautiful and terrifying and her best friend. She didn't doubt his love for her, just as she knew she loved him. However, both were fully aware that this was as much as they would have together; a deeply caring friendship and they provided what the other needed. Terric demanded Jordyn stay connected and allowed her to feel. She provided Terric a physical outlet for his sexual nature, his dominance, and protecting her fulfilled a need he didn't even know he had. Being steady for her forced him to keep himself level.

Terric didn't allow himself to explore his sexuality. He kept his preferences under lock and key. In fact, Jordyn was the only being alive who knew that Terric preferred men to women, and only because he refused to lie to her. From the first day, he'd made it clear that he was incapable of taking her for a mate. Instead, he would protect her from the advances of others, from the outside world completely, and swore to never hurt her or lead her on. All the while, he staved off questions about his personal life. Their arrangement worked. For now.

Chapter Two

THE FIRST COUPLE of weeks in the club went as expected. Terric's presence was resented at first, until he had cleared out the employees who were an obvious problem. He hadn't seen much of Lucas after the first couple of days. For now, he was focusing on the club, learning the clientele and the staff. Later, he would spend some time in Trespass, the other half of Lucas and Victoria's little empire.

Terric had met with a couple of Provincetown's finest. Taking time to acquaint himself with the local police was important in his line of work. The two he met seemed decent enough; one was human, and one was a vampire. The area had that small town feel, and meeting with the two of them confirmed his assumptions. Ptown not a high crime area, but it had its share of action.

He sat in a booth, listening to them describe the facility that had been constructed to house creatures such as himself that crossed the line. Unsure if they were issuing him a warning or simply proud of what they had accomplished, he still felt impressed. In one relatively small compound-like facility they were able to arrest and house a suspect in a holding area, try him, and then imprison him, all without leaving that set of buildings. The prison was constructed with the unique needs of containing supernatural beings in mind. It contained interrogation rooms, holding cells, and lockups designed for longer stays. Out of necessity, also included was an area that dealt with execution, accomplished in any manner that may be needed, depending on the being. All of these areas, if viewed with human use in mind, would seem barbaric and akin to sheer torture. But they were necessary for accommodating the special abilities of Provincetown's otherworlder population. He agreed to tour the facility within the next few days and thanked them for their time before returning to work.

Terric walked outside, doing a pass around the parking lot and taking in some fresh air. He had been restless lately, his wolf pacing and straining to be allowed to run. He took deep breaths, forcing that side of him to settle for a while longer. Soon, when he knew he had some privacy, he would allow himself to shift and give himself over to the animal completely. He came around the corner of the building, his senses sharpening as he smelled the coppery hint of fresh blood. Human blood. He stopped, taking in the scene before him. The town was safer than most, but not immune to violence.

A human, barely older than a kid, was getting his ass kicked by a shifter. The shifter was playing with the boy. A human was no match for his superior strength, regardless of age or size. Terric dug into the shifter's mind and nearly recoiled at the blackness he found there. As a demon, Terric was charged with taking souls and bringing them to his boss, in the other realm. The demon master was a sick, sadistic fuck, just like the shifter standing before him.

The shifter enjoyed the pain and fear the human was radiating. The shifter's arousal didn't come from sexual attraction to the human, but from causing agony in a weaker opponent. He thrived on it, looked for any excuse. In this case, the human had told him he could find the shifter any connections in the local high school, both in dealing drugs and with underage girls. Seemed the shifter had an interest in both, and the kid delivered neither. He had developed a conscience and had come to tell the shifter he changed his mind. The shifter wasn't interested in the kid's excuses, and the punishment had commenced.

Terric surged forward, not sure what he was going to do. His usual instinct would be to steal the fucker's soul, but he didn't do that with shifters. He hated the idea of trapping an animal in that realm, forever in between, no escape. Even if the shifter's other form was truly evil, he couldn't condemn an animal to that fate. He usually just exterminated them. Far kinder that way; quick, painless and efficient. This time, however, T really hoped the male fought back. He needed it tonight.

Stepping out of the shadows, he saw the shifter turn at once, his senses as keen as Terric's. He tossed the human aside like refuse, the kid hit the wall hard, the sound of his head on the bricks was loud, a dull thud. The kid was out, blood pooling around his head. He was alive, but unconscious. Terric approached the shifter, burrowing deeper into the male's mind. He tried to numb the bear spirit inside the man, ease what lay ahead. He couldn't go too far with that, however. He wanted there to be suffering for the man, retribution.

Soundlessly, he misted directly behind the male, gripping his opponent's head firmly in his large hands. He held there for a moment before his mouth dropped down to the man's flesh, lips resting for a moment in almost a caress, tasting the skin and inhaling the scent. He opened his mouth, sharp canines throbbing as he sank his teeth into the thickly muscled neck and his grip on the man's head tightened. The bite wasn't necessary; he simply indulged that side of his nature that enjoyed causing deserved pain. With a quick jerk of his hands, Terric snapped the man's neck, nearly an internal decapitation. He soundlessly dragged the body behind the dumpster and immolated the carcass with nothing more than a thought and a nudge of energy.

Terric was scarcely breathing hard when he approached the human kid. He stood over the unconscious form, coolly assessing the kid's injuries. The bleeding had stopped. As head wounds tend to do, it had bled profusely for a time, but the injury wasn't life threatening, so he merely rearranged some memories in the kid's brain, taking some details and replacing them with others. The kid was going to wake up piss-his-pants terrified, convinced that his current condition had resulted from partying too hard with some tourists, a combination of drinking too much, going on a bad trip, and the tourists kicking his ass and humiliating him. Hopefully, making him think twice before dabbling in illegal shit again.

Terric pulled the kid's body over by the surveillance cameras so he could keep a distant eye on him and left him in the alley, turning and heading back into the club. He worked in his office, going through invoices and making notes on purchasing patterns of the club over the past several months. Every so often, he would check the cameras to see if the kid was doing okay. When the kid started to rouse, he had gone out to the alley once more, checked his pockets for a wallet, and called a cab. He made sure the cabbie was one of the regulars that had brought several of his customers home safely. He found the kid's information on his license. He gave the driver the address from the kid's license with strict instructions to see the kid, Devon Cole, home safely to his parents. He gave the driver the fare along with a generous tip and his own phone number to call if any problems arose.

Terric headed back inside, closing the door to his office once more in a bid for quiet. He finished going over the invoices, loaded the information into a spreadsheet program, and then generated some graphs to go over later. It seemed Ascendance had been doing everything the old fashioned way, which normally he favored himself. Nowadays, however, it was important to be able to do both, understand the information, and grab a visual representation of necessary information. He was still learning the ins and outs of the computer and its various programs, but he enjoyed the preciseness of it.

T glanced over at his phone to check the time, noting the club would soon be closing. He stood, stretching his arms over his head and rolling his shoulders to work the kinks out. When he left his office, he walked several paces to the bar on the main floor. Willow was working it. Normally, she worked the VIP area exclusively. She was the bar manager, had been there since Vickie and Lucas had opened. A fallen angel, as beautiful as she was sweet, Willow had a mischievous streak a mile wide.

She winked at him as he approached, deftly taking a tip from a human that no doubt figured she was as in love with him as he was with her, if the fifty she threw in the tip bucket was any indication. He asked her how the night was going, and her reply was saucy as usual. "Sheer Heaven, Wolfie, and I would know." She flashed her trademark smile that hinted at both unblemished innocence and outrageous sensuality then returned her attention to the straggling patrons, urging them to finish their drinks and head out.

He had wondered if she would have issue with his heritage. She was fine with him though, having grown used to it with Lucas. Willow understood the fact that demons were as much a necessity as angels. She had an easygoing nature regardless, and he was glad she had stayed on when many of her coworkers had either quit or been fired. Still, he noticed she tended to call him Wolf—Wolfie when she was being playful—or simply T, as if to separate him a bit from the demon side of what he was. He didn't mind; often he tried to do the same.

T waited several minutes to make sure the big spender didn't hang out, expecting something in return for the large tip. The man left after blowing Willow several noisy kisses. Terric laughed and continued to make the rounds of the club. Once the place was empty of patrons and ready for the cleaning crew to come in, he headed out to the parking lot, doing a final check before heading to his truck.

The plan was to head home, but the windows were down, and the tang of sea air had Terric heading to the beach instead. He parked and sat, debating. Finally, he dug out his phone and sent a text to Jordyn, letting her know he wouldn't be home for a while. He needed distance. The life he was living wore on him sometimes. His life had a necessary rhythm, but at times, it became an oppressive metronome, the monotony of which threatened to suffocate him. He had nothing he could point at and know that was what he strove for, and maybe that was the problem. If a benchmark for success didn't exist for him, then he had nothing to achieve.

His life was static; he was static. He left his truck and hit the boardwalk, heading for the sand. The beach shimmered, looking almost silver where the moon reflected off the water.

He found himself sitting on the damp sand, studying the lighthouse. The beacon swept across the land, over the dunes, and then out to sea, another metronome of a sort. This one comforted him. He felt something inside himself settle. Observing the way the light danced on the waves and made them glow, he was reminded of the bioluminescence seen in other bodies of water he had studied. Always, he watched alone. The solitude had never bothered him, and it hadn't occurred to him to bring Jordyn.

This type of quiet was not something she was comfortable with, and he couldn't share his thoughts with her. Not the ones that assaulted him at these times when he was still, surrounded by beauty but unable to truly see it. The vastness of the sea and the light that cut into the darkness showed him that nothing was out there, nothing that was his.

A whale breached the surface, punctuating the action by blowing air through his blowholes. Most likely a humpback, common around Cape Cod. The haunting song identified it as a male, and Terric wondered if the creature was lonely or in the middle of trying to secure a mate. He watched it skimming along the surface, seeming to play within the light provided by the lighthouse's beacon. Finally, it left, and Terric was alone once more.

He stood, swiped his hands down his jeans to dislodge the

damp sand before heading back to his truck and driving home. He let himself into the apartment and headed directly for the balcony. Sleep wasn't going to happen. As he sat there on the rickety lawn chair the previous tenant had left behind, it occurred to him that he might be better off buying a house. Something near the water where he could maybe see the lighthouse, while also able to protect Jordy from the sun.

She loved the water at night, and watching her in the waves was fucking magic. Her body, taut and perfect, moved sinuously as if she were a mythical creature that existed to lure hapless sea captains into the ocean's depths. The blonde waves that tumbled down her back darkened and nearly reached her ass, winding around her as she moved. That image of her was one of several seared into his brain, one of the rare times her smile reached her eyes.

THE SUN PINKENED the horizon, and the sounds of the neighborhood starting to awaken and move about rose up to greet him. Terric could hear someone admonish their dog to be patient, then clip a leash on it, and head off jogging. Someone else dragged a garbage can across pavement, the metal grating on the concrete an insult in the early morning stillness. He slowly stood up, stretched, and looked once more at the sky. The sun was coming up, and the moon was still visible. He had always loved seeing that for some reason. He turned and headed into the apartment, locking the door firmly behind him and then pulling the blackout shade in case Jordy wandered through. She usually did before heading to bed. She would be restless and tended to pace a bit before settling down.

Jordyn was readying for bed, a large towel wrapped turban-like around her head, wearing a pair of skimpy panties with one of his tee shirts. T walked over, kissed her full lips, and then drew her over to the bed. He massaged her head, drying her hair with the towel before slowly unwinding it. He rose briefly, dropped it on the hamper in the bathroom as he grabbed her brush, and silently re-entered the room. He began untangling the long, thick mass of hair. She relaxed her spine and rested her hands on his knees as he settled in behind her. He continued brushing in long, smooth strokes. The tangles were gone, but the act relaxed her, and he loved the scent of her fresh from her bath. Jordy sighed softly and he grinned, knowing she was enjoying his touch and attention.

They talked about nothing for a while, just the random things one shares that are safe and not likely to lead to other topics. Before long they had settled in, Terric's arm lying lightly on Jordyn's waist as she lay facing away from him. Eventually, her breathing evened out, and he slowed his to match hers, relaxing into a light sleep. The patterns of their days were becoming the same as they had been before they moved to Provincetown, the routine comfortable to them both and essential to Jordy.

JORDYN WOKE, HER dreams mocking her once again. She had heard a baby cry and had risen to investigate. She had padded from room to room, increasingly frantic, looking for her child. Her breasts had felt heavy, as they had before, a signal to nurse. The apartment wasn't that large and nothing like her old one, not really. But for some reason, she couldn't separate the two. She had become confused, and had started running back and forth, the carpet silencing the sound of her bare feet along the hallway. Her hair hung in her face, sweat coated her skin in a fine sheen, and finally, she crumbled to the floor, her eyes staring blindly at the wall.

JORDY HAD NO idea how long she lay there and considered calling out to Terric to come help her. She knew she was dangerously close to the edge. Much further and she wouldn't be able to pull herself back. She allowed herself to feel the agony, and then she stiffened her spine, forcing herself to sit straight. She sat there, changing the inner monologue forcefully. For every horrible thought she had about herself, she made herself think of a good quality she had. Self-healing was something new for her.

Normally, Terric would help her through this. If she froze, unable to communicate at all, he would systematically tear down every wall she put up until she was reduced to a crying, hysterical mess. At that point, he would step in, scoop her up, and hold her. And he would tell her all the good things he saw in her, his baritone voice a soothing monotone. It would take a long time before she would even hear his words, so lost in the past and the storm tearing through her soul.

THIS TIME, THOUGH, she took herself to their playroom. And instead of having Terric use the various instruments on her body until she broke, she simply walked around and looked at everything. Her wide gaze took in each and every object he had ever touched against her body. The various floggers and the whips were arranged on the wall in order of severity of possible pain inflicted, and shackles hung from brackets screwed into the wall. Masks were displayed, but mainly for show. Terric disliked using them on her; he needed to be able to see her face to gauge where she was at all times, both physically and mentally.

This level of play was not something Terric would have done, normally. He did it for her, and that was it. She knew that, and it bothered her to think that he would prefer not to engage in this lifestyle. He was dominant by nature, and his preferences did not lean toward the vanilla in any way. But she could see that, although he excelled at taking command of her body, he did not need it in the way she did. He did not like causing her actual pain. Her vampire senses were as acute as his demon ones, and she could feel him fighting with himself, struggling with the idea of marking her skin.

Jordyn didn't want to need this. She wondered if it were something she would have sought had her life taken a different course. She approached the wall where the harnesses and rope hung, grabbed a length of rope and gracefully lowered herself to sit on the floor where she sat for a long time, considering her life. Her hands played with the rope, absentmindedly tying it into knots, untying it, and starting over. Eventually, when her eyes started to drift closed, she returned the rope to the wall and headed back to bed.

A COUPLE HOURS later, Terric awoke on his back with Jordyn resting her cheek on the dip of his shoulder, her golden hair spread over his arm. He couldn't see her face, but her breathing told him she was awake and not doing well. He wordlessly reached down and slid his palm over her head, smoothing the hair off her face. At his touch, she took a shuddering breath, and he felt his skin dampen from the hot tears that streamed out of her eyes. He didn't say anything for a while, just kept stroking her, waiting until she was ready to talk.

Finally, she began, her voice soft but picking up strength. "I'm sorry. For dragging you into this life with me. I know you aren't happy either, even though you pretend everything is fine, that all is as it should be. I hate what I've become. And I hate that neither of us is living the life we should be living. You need to be honest about who and what you are. And I need to be honest, too, and strong enough to admit that I am lost. You're my best friend, and I love you. I'm just... so afraid. Afraid to feel and afraid not to, you know?"

Terric burrowed his hand into her hair, fingers resting against the nape of her neck, and eased her head back until she was looking into his eyes. "You okay? Do you need me to take you to the playroom, Jordyn?"

Her eyes were strong, focused on his, as she answered softly, "No, Terric. Truly, I'm fine. I'm pretty proud of myself, actually. I did this alone, went in there and just sat, thought, and cried. So no. I want to see how far I can go on my own right now. I'm tired and going to sleep for a little while... Tomorrow I will finish the unpacking and work more on setting the place up. It's good, really. Finally, some progress."

Terric eased his hand out from her hair, being careful not to pull on it as it tangled around his fingers. A surge of pride went through him, and he smiled down at her, gently kissing her lips. "Good girl, you let me know, though, okay? If that changes. And as far as the rest of it, stop. Stop worrying about me and whether or not I'm happy. Do I strike you as the type to do anything I don't want to do? I love you. That's enough. The rest doesn't matter. Who lives the life they are supposed to be living, anyways? Does anyone even know what that is? Besides, look at me! I'm an anomaly. A fucking bisexual demon shifter. Not really all of any one thing. What kind of life could I lead? I don't really fit in most categories, you know." He paused, feeling the truth in that sentence. "No. I'm where I should be. You're right, we should sleep. We have a lot to do tomorrow."

Chapter Three

JORDYN WAS LIVID. Terric had not brought any of their old furniture from New York. She had thought most of it was in storage, but no. He had announced that they had to go shopping for new things. He had assured her that he had put all her personal things from... before, into storage, but the furniture, all of it, was gone. Fresh start, he had said. Didn't he understand? She didn't deserve a fresh start; her parents and brother wouldn't ever have that opportunity ever again. Her child, her baby, had never had any start at all. They had been robbed of life because of choices she had made.

She needed the reminders, needed to see the familiar things around her all the time; things that she had been staring at for years. At first, she had hated all of Terric's furniture. The dark masculinity of it had made it hard for her to breathe. Then she fell in love with it for precisely that reason. It made her uncomfortable, and that was perfect; she didn't deserve comfort. When he had told her the furnishings were gone, she had turned on her heel and walked away. After she didn't return, he had gone searching for her, and when she refused to look him in the face, tonelessly telling him she was fine, he had stood over her and glared, waiting with infinite patience for her to elaborate. "I'm fine. I just want to be alone, please," she had said, her voice a strained whisper. She refused to raise her eyes until he had gripped her chin firmly and forced her to meet his gaze. Her eyes had shone with unshed tears, and she blinked rapidly, hating herself for feeling as if she had the right to cry. They were not even her things, and if he wanted to toss them out, he had that right. If he wanted to get rid of *her*, that was also his right. She didn't know why he didn't, truthfully.

Jordyn felt a sharp pain, like the mental version of a bee sting. Fuck. He was doing it. He was in her head, picking through her thoughts. He almost never did that. He hated it more than the people he did it to. It exhausted him, pissed him off. He only did it when he felt he had no other choice. She knew then she must look awful. She drew in a deep breath, forcing herself to relax and allow his invasion. The tears started to flow freely now. "I'm sorry, Terric." After several moments, she felt him withdraw. She exhaled and glanced over at him, her hands folded in her lap as she sat, her legs drawn up under her.

"JORDY, THEY'RE JUST things. Inanimate objects. We don't need them here. This is a new life, for both of us. We'll go shopping, and you will pick out things you like. It's time, baby. You have been doing so well, so much better. And you will do this. There is no room for discussion. It's not up for debate. The shit is gone, donated. And what little we brought, that you see around you now, that is getting donated as well." His voice was firm, cold even.

If he eased up on her, if she sensed he was weakening, she would pounce on it; try to finagle her own way. And he would end up tracking down all the donated shit and trying to buy it all back. He had to distance himself from her for a little while. The devastated look in her eyes would have him caving. The progress she had made last night made standing his ground now even harder, but that much more important as well. "I'll be back in a couple of hours. Be ready to go."

Terric drove the truck around, not heading anywhere in particular. He ended up stopping at a neighborhood bar called Mulligan's. He walked in, noting its small, dim interior—the kind of place he preferred. He nodded to a couple of the patrons as he walked by them, their curious stares nothing more than he was used to. The customers were mainly humans, save for two otherworlders. Male shifters. Wolf, like him, evident by their scent and the way his wolf became more alert.

He ordered a beer from the waiting bartender and lifted it to the shifters in a toast, an acknowledgment and affirmation he was one of them. Still, he headed over to the opposite end of the bar, pulled out a chair, and sat, pretending to give a shit about the game on the big screen. He wasn't surprised when one of them came over, gesturing to the seat next to him. He shrugged, not wanting to engage in small talk. The guy had other ideas, it seemed.

He sat and stuck his hand out to shake. Said his name was Kevin, and at the table was his brother, Seth. Terric flicked a glance over at the brother, noting the guy's surly, pissed off expression. He almost preferred that to the open friendliness of Kevin. At least he understood it better. Who did that? Walked around and introduced themselves, made small talk with strangers?

Belatedly, he realized the guy still had a hold of his hand, his stomach did a strange little twist and he pulled his hand back. The guy laughed lightly, and apologized. He didn't appear sorry though. He looked... hungry. Kevin's face was tan, as if he spent most of his time outdoors. He was fit, not overly muscled in an artificial way. It didn't look like Kevin spent time working out at some gym, but he clearly got a daily work out. Terric frowned, wondering what the guy's deal was, and why it mattered. Kevin called over to the bartender, ordered another round for both of them, and had it put on his tab. Terric thanked him, and picked up the beer, trying to figure out a way to ease away from the strange male. The guy was making him feel wrong, off. T stared into his grayish blue eyes, trying to see what was going on, without actually having to get inside his head. Nothing. He dug a little deeper and then deeper still.

The guy's mind was unlike anything he had ever experienced before. Open and just... caring. As if he had missed out on the fact that the world sucked, and people were not good and kind. It felt nice in there, clean. He found that he didn't want to leave, wanted to wander around in there, learn this male, inside and out. And then he saw what the male was feeling for him. Desire. This male, Kevin, desired Terric. Wanted to touch him, talk to him, and hold him. And yeah, being a male, wanted to fuck him.

Not going to fucking happen. Terric stood abruptly. He was furious. He dropped his gaze as he felt his eyes change. This was not the place to cause a scene, all the humans milling about. Besides, the guy hadn't technically done anything wrong, hadn't acted inappropriately. But he knew. This Kevin knew what Terric was. He sensed Terric's attraction to him and he knew that Terric would be tempted to step into the fantasy, to touch and be touched.

Terric set down his mostly untouched beer, the noise of it hitting the bar loud in his ears. Kevin looked at him strangely, clueless that Terric had just thoroughly invaded his privacy. That surprised Terric, but then, Kevin wouldn't recognize it if he hadn't experienced it before. Once more, he reminded himself that the guy had done nothing wrong and forced himself to be civil. "I just realized how late it was man, sorry. I have to get my female, promised to take her shopping. We just moved here. I'm running Ascendance and don't have many nights off. I'll see you around." He shook the guy's hand, nodded at the brother, and got the hell out. He could feel Kevin's confusion and refused to feel bad about it. He also refused to dwell on the fact that he had memorized Kevin's features, and his eyes had traveled more than once over Kevin's body, noting the contrast between the dark brown hair and light eyes that sparked with humor.

What the fuck? Why had he told him where he was working? Almost as if he wanted the guy to come find him. T quickly dismissed the thought, placing the blame on Jordyn and the shit she had been talking about the night before. He unlocked his truck, starting it and sitting there for a few minutes. His life felt out of control. Too much was changing at once, as if he were on the edge of something, and once it started, he would be powerless to rein it in.

THE RIDE TO the mall was quiet, but Jordyn seemed calmer. Terric let her have her space, using the time to try to settle his own nerves. He kept replaying that meeting with Kevin in his mind. He parked the truck, walking around to her side and opening her door. His hand rested on the small of her back as they entered the building, and he made eye contact with every male that turned to stare at her. His lip pulled back off his teeth, revealing a sharp canine to one human man that dared eye-fuck her while she stopped to look in the window of some clothing store. The human took one glance at Terric and abruptly changed course, heading in the opposite direction with sudden purpose.

They continued through to the furniture store, one of several in the mall. Terric realized Jordyn was hanging back, staring at him expectantly. He stroked her arm gently. "Pick whatever you like, Jordy. You choose. I'm fine with whatever you want." She smiled and started to walk ahead of him. After about fifteen minutes of wandering, she began to grow upset. He watched her face intently, ready to take her out of the store quickly if she needed him to.

She walked around the store faster, looking at everything for a few seconds before moving on. Then she would double back, frustration beginning to show. On her third pass around the same display, he stepped in front of her, grabbing her hand in his. She stopped, but otherwise ignored him. Her gaze was fixed over his shoulder, examining the entire store a piece at a time. Terric took her face in his hands, forcing her to look at him. When she did, her eyes welled up, one tear slipping down her face. He caught it with his thumb. His voice was a gentle whisper. "What's going on, baby? Talk to me. Where are you at right now?"

Jordyn's voice was a plaintive cry, the corners of her sensual mouth turned down. She seemed both overwhelmed and defeated. "I don't know what I like. And I can't remember if I ever did know. What the hell is wrong with me that I don't even know how to pick out furniture? How can I ever be normal when I don't even know which color is my favorite? Or what styles I like? I don't know anything about me! I must bore the fuck out of you... I'm nothing. There is nothing interesting about me. I just reflect the people around me. I can't even remember what food tastes like or what my favorite fruit is. Jesus, I'm sick of myself. How can you not be tired of me?"

Terric let go of her face, wrapped his arms around her, and pulled her to him, rubbing her back in a slow, comforting circle. He spoke softly in her ear, his voice soothing and calm. "I love you, Jordyn. For all the things that I see in you that you just can't see right now. You may not be aware of all your preferences, but that is another example of the kind of person you are. You have never made yourself a priority, and you need to. You are kind, strong, and loving. Your spirit is beautiful, and it shines so damn bright it's blinding. I'm humbled every time I wake up and see you. I remember what you've gone through, and I am amazed at your strength. I have seen every manner of depravity and all kinds of evil. You lived with it, lived through it. And even after all that, you still have the ability to love, to forgive, to heal. You can do this. I'll help you. For now, we'll pick out the basics. We can do the rest together later, okay? We can buy a bed and some stuff to hold us a couple weeks while we work on this. No rush."

Jordyn stood in his arms, letting his strength fill her. After a long moment, she nodded and pulled back. Terric wiped the tears from her face and took her hand; their fingers interlaced, and led her throughout the store. They went to the mattresses, testing out different models. She couldn't figure out if she truly liked the harder ones or the soft ones and to head off any further issues, Terric ordered a Sleep Number and one of the Tempur-Pedic ones. They could figure it out later, and the number one would make it easy for her to figure out what she liked. She could easily adjust it.

As they were leaving, he would point out a piece of furniture to her and see what she thought. To his amusement, she was able to tell him what she hated, and it seemed they had vastly different tastes. It would truly be interesting to see what she finally ended up picking out for their place.

They stopped at a restaurant. Terric ordered a beer and nachos while Jordyn got a glass of white wine and a salad. Neither was very hungry, but it was good to be out of the house together. Terric told her more about his work, the people he had met. He even told her a bit about Devon, the kid who had stuck in his head. Jordyn was distracted but calm; her mind was still going over the shopping trip.

When they were back in the truck and headed home, she quietly told him she needed to feed soon. He nodded, said that was fine. Feeding her was always strange for him. The plain fact was that she needed blood to live. He wasn't a vampire, but she could exist off his blood. Another vampire would perhaps have been better for her, but he would never allow anyone else to feed her. She was too vulnerable during those times. That was one of the ways her mate had fucked with her, one of the many unthinkable ways. Terric had to prepare himself to feed her by thoroughly burying his dominant nature and let her completely take control. They had figured it all out, together, over the years. What worked best for her, what she could deal with. When they arrived home, they sat on the balcony for a while before he stood, kissed her mouth softly, and told her he was going in to prepare.

Terric stood in the shower for a few minutes, forcing his mind to go blank. He washed his body, removing all traces of the day, wanting to be as clean as possible for her. He had a hard time thinking of her taking his demon blood into her perfect body. She had assured him that she loved his taste and that she was fine with the fact that he was a demon. It was a fact about himself that he tolerated only because he had no choice. He didn't bother wishing things were different, except for the times when she needed to take him into her body for sustenance. He tried not to become aroused when she fed from him, which was difficult. Feeding was an intimate, sensual act.

He leaned against the wall, the spray hitting him and pouring over his body as he palmed his still soapy cock, his eyes closing as he began to masturbate. He stroked himself from the base to the head, slowly at first, twisting his wrist when he reached the tip. His other hand dropped the soap and reached down to cup his balls, his sac tightening as he came closer to climaxing. His breathing accelerated, images flashing in his mind. Jordyn's perfect body against his, driving inside her heat while he palmed one perfect breast and took the other in his mouth. He exploded, coming in spurts that hit the wall of the shower. The fact that during his orgasm Jordyn's image was replaced by a man with light eyes, dark hair and a body that piqued his interest was something he would worry about later.

He moved under the spray, recovering and washing his body once more. It never helped entirely, but it took the edge off the fact that he would want to bury himself inside her as she sank those pretty little fangs into his flesh. Terric stepped from the shower, grabbing a towel and quickly dried before drawing on a pair of jeans. He swiped the towel over his head to dry his hair and then slung it over his shoulders before heading to the balcony and opening the sliding glass door. Jordyn turned and looked at him expectantly. "I'm ready. Meet you there in a minute, okay?" At her nod, he shut the door and headed to the playroom.

This was the part that tended to fuck with Terric's head. He rolled his shoulders a few times, took several deep breaths. Hanging his towel on a hook by the door, he forced himself to calm. He lay down on the floor, the safest place if he did panic during any of this. It had only happened once, but it had shaken him to the core to realize he could have hurt her by throwing her off of him. He relaxed his spine, aligning his body and stretching out his arms and legs. The legs used to be restrained straight, but they found it harder for him to resist and potentially break the restraints if his legs were spread open. His heartbeat quickened, and he closed his eyes, breathing in through his nose and out through his mouth. This feeling, this helpless feeling, fucked with Terric, remind-ed him of the time he spent down in the other realm, vulnerable to all the invasions inflicted upon a demon called to task down there.

Jordyn needed this. She couldn't feel safe and feed if he weren't restrained. She had to know that no one would touch her during it; no one would force her or hurt her in anyway. Even then, simply taking in needed sustenance remained brutally difficult for her. This act, a biological necessity for her, had been used as a weapon against her.

Jordyn had been nearly dead when he found her, had grown even closer to death as she refused to feed. He had nearly forced her in an act of desperation when she finally had broken and told him why she couldn't do it. It had been during a particularly harsh session; Terric had come perilously close to losing patience with her and it had shaken him. He was sickened that there had been anger behind the hand driving the whip, flicking relentlessly against her creamy skin.

He had thrown it down, horrified at himself. She had finally cried, and the story came pouring out of her in a burst of hysterical tears. He had had such a hard time understanding her that he had simply delved into her mind instead, to see the memory for himself. His mind had recoiled from the evil that she had been subjected to. No, this was nothing compared to what she had endured. He could deal with being restrained by the shackle of her choice. She deserved to feed in relative peace.

Jordyn entered the room, shyly standing just inside the door. She glanced at Terric, limbs akimbo while he waited for her. Her eyes traveled over his body, lean yet muscular. Powerful. The knowledge that he suffered doing this tore at her. She moved closer to him, snagging the large bondage cuffs and the leather tethers that attached to them. She knelt beside him, laying a hand on his cheek until he opened his eyes then leaned down, kissed his cheek softly, and whispered, "I'm sorry" to him. He nodded, unspeaking, and closed his eyes again.

Jordyn moved to first one arm and then the other, buckling the cuff on his wrists and repeating the process at his ankles. She paused for a moment, checking her anxiety level. An idea occurred to her, and she let the thought run through her head to see how she felt about it. Terric opened his eyes once more, peering at her curiously. Finally, he told her to finish it, finish putting the restraints on him. She heard the stress in his voice and felt bad for drawing it out. "No, T. I want to try something. I want to try doing this without all that. I'll leave the cuffs on, but just that, a step toward being able to feed normally. Can I do that? Do you mind if I try?"

Terric's tone was cautious, his voice patient. "I don't mind, baby, but you don't need to. I'm fine. This way worked for so long, I see no reason to change it." He lay there, unmoving, while she examined her feelings.

Finally, she gave a shaky smile and shook her head. "No, I'm good. I feel strong, and I want to try it. Don't move though, okay?" At his nod, she sat beside him, crossing her legs as he closed his eyes once more. She stared down at him, taking in his features and memorizing them in case other images tried to take over once she started. Her hand reached out and stroked him, starting at his chest above his sternum. She stroked her fingertips lightly over the fire brand that marked him as demon.

When he was summoned, it grew warm, nearly hot enough to burn her flesh at times. She had felt it before. He had been summoned, and she had gone to him, hugging him. Her palm had rested over his heart and then moved upwards slightly, only to jerk away in shock. She had touched him again, intrigued and horrified, until his palm had flattened over her hand and drew it away. It didn't today; he let her explore.

Her fingers played across his six-pack, over his flat abdomen, and down, moving to his side and over his flank to rest on his hip. She loved the way he felt, the difference between him and the way her mate had felt. Terric was leaner, harder, but her fingers delighted at the feel of his skin and the way he trembled when she caressed his stomach. Ticklish. No one would have believed her, that the demon had many such ticklish areas.

She felt herself warming, relaxing, and her body began to ready itself for both feeding and sex. Her fangs throbbed, wanting so badly to bury inside his vein, and her sex grew wet. Images of her straddling him while he thrust himself inside her took over her thoughts. Terric groaned her name, warningly. Her imaginings must have been loud, and vivid, if she had broadcast them directly into his mind. She felt him stiffen, trying to deny his body's growing arousal. She apologized and tried to focus.

This hadn't been an issue before. She had always focused on the feeding and getting it over with. She felt curiously empowered though, more so than before when he had been rendered completely immobile. The sense of danger remained, yes, but laced with an edge of excitement.

Finally, she leaned forward, her chest pressed into his as she nuzzled at his neck. His head was angled away to give her the access she needed, and she found the vein she was seeking. Her lips caressed the skin for a moment, and then she sucked in hard, readying the area before she struck sharply. He jolted slightly and then relaxed as she drew his blood from him, drinking slowly this time. She allowed herself time to savor his flavor, the feeling of power and strength she took from him.

Her small hand reached out and rested lightly on his stomach, wanting desperately to move lower. He would never have sex with her during a feeding, so her hand remained where it was. The ache grew, though, to have such a connection to someone and not fear it. She opened her eyes, moving her head slightly to check his face. Other than a fine sheen of sweat covering his skin, she couldn't see much. Dissatisfied, she closed her eyes and returned her attention to feeding, taking longer and harder draws. This was the point where she would be reaching orgasm, if she had been able to do this normally. Finally sated, she withdrew from him, placing an openmouthed kiss on the puncture marks, slowing and then stopping the blood loss.

Jordyn sat back, proud of herself. Her eyes were shining when they met his, and she saw the strained expression on his face. His breathing was slowing, but she could still see beads of sweat on his brow. Her gaze swept down his body and stopped on his obvious erection. He was so hard it must have been painful. She glanced into his eyes, and he looked ashamed. "What's wrong, Terric? It went so well. I thought you'd be happy…"

Terric cleared his throat, finally drawing a full breath. He was still lying there, spread out before her. He wouldn't move until he was sure she was okay with things. "I am happy, baby. You did great. I'm sorry, about that." With a nod, he indicated his erection. "I need to get up and be away from you for a minute. Okay, baby?"

"I want you to get up, yeah. But I don't want you to go take care of that. I want to. I want you in my mouth, and I want you inside me. Now, please." Jordyn's voice had lost its shyness. She met his stare, her lips parted as she imagined him surging into her mouth, swallowing him. She hurriedly unbuckled the wrist and ankle cuffs and dropped them on the floor. Even though they hadn't been tethered, she wanted them off…

He sat up, reflexively rubbing at his wrists and watching

her, gauging her emotional state. Jordyn caught his hesitation and leaned forward, her lips parting as they met his and her tongue already licking at him. Terric's breathing accelerated, and his arms went around her, pulling her against his body and deepening the kiss. They stayed like that for several moments, until he remembered where they were. He stood, offering a hand to her and helping her up. Jordyn wrapped her body around him, her hand stroking him outside his jeans until he picked her up, her legs wrapping around his waist as he held her against him and carried her to his room.

She remained that way, entwined around him, his hands gripping her ass as he moved his lips to her neck. She made an impatient noise, her legs leaving his waist as she stood in front of him before going lithely to her knees as her hands unzipped his jeans. She had her mouth on him as she pulled the denim down over his hips, his hands burying in her hair and cupping the back of her head. Terric stared down at her, the sight nearly bringing him to climax. Her gaze met his as her tongue played around the head of his cock, running down the shaft and back up, swirling around the sensitive underside as she closed her lips around him.

He had to close his eyes for a moment, calling on all his control to not thrust deep inside her, down her throat, and climax immediately. When Terric's eyes opened, he looked down once more at her face, his hips thrusting his cock in and out of her willing mouth steadily until he could take no more. He lowered himself to the floor, on his knees facing her. His hands peeled her shirt off, opening the front closure of her bra and cupping her breasts, his thumbs moving over the sensitive nipples. Jordyn let out a soft moan, her head tilting back, causing her flaxen hair to brush the floor.

Terric quickly dispatched the remainder of her clothes, easing her onto her back. He stared down at her, sitting on his haunches as he gazed at her naked body. He gently eased her legs apart, spreading her open before him. He moved no closer to her, staying where he was so he could watch her face as he traced a finger lightly over her mound and then parted her folds with his thumbs before easing a finger into her. She tried to close her eyes, a light blush on her cheeks as she began to pant slightly.

"Open your eyes, baby. Now. I am going to watch you, watch your face as you orgasm. You're so close, pretty baby. Even now, you're so tight on my finger. You feel so good. Relax, open yourself up to me. You're so tight. I can see it on your face as I ease the second finger in. It stretches, doesn't it, baby? It doesn't hurt, though. You love it." As she nodded, her breath came faster and her eyes tried to drift closed. "Jordy, eyes on me. Don't close me out. Good, that's my good girl. I'm going to put my mouth on you now, taste you. I want those eyes open, you understand me?"

She nodded once more, her voice a breathless whisper. "Yes, Terric, I understand. Please… oh…" She trailed off, not even sure what she was asking for. He seemed to understand, though. His voice was smug, confident. "I have you, baby. I'm right here." Terric lowered himself to his stomach, lying between her open legs, and dropped his mouth to her, his breath hot on her skin as he withdrew his fingers for a moment.

Jordyn gave a little whimper, wanting them back inside her, and he stroked her hip and murmured to her before once more spreading her open and running his tongue lightly from her tiny opening to her clit, back and forth until she began to move her hips restlessly. His eyes flew to her face to ensure she was doing as she had been told and that her eyes were open. Terric gave her a small grin and a nod, acknowledging her compliance. He focused back on her body, and bringing her to climax. His tongue entered the narrow opening, fucking into her as she screamed, and he tasted her orgasm. His finger entered her as well, and her walls immediately clamped down on it, spasming around him, and he kept his pace and pressure steady, letting her set the tone and move as she needed to. Sounds of approval left him as she continued to climax for several moments.

Finally, she came down from it, her body still trembling. Her eyes drifted closed, and Terric allowed it for the moment, giving her time to compose herself as he moved up her body. He lined himself up with her, nudging her thighs farther apart with his hips, and surged into her in one sharp thrust. Immediately, he began to move inside her as she felt another orgasm building, her legs moving to lock around his waist as he fucked her hard. Terric saw no sign of trepidation in her. In fact, she began to urge him to fuck her harder, faster.

He let himself loosen his iron control, gripping her hips roughly to hold her in place as he began to nearly rut on top of her, the slap of their bodies loud in his ears. Terric yelled her name, urging her to come again. And she obeyed once more, screaming as she felt her orgasm grip her, sending a tingling sensation from her lower back, along every nerve ending, through the rest of her body. She was incapable of rational thought as she became a mass of sensation. As Terric felt her go over the edge, he joined her. His body thrust several more times until he pressed himself deep inside her, his seed filling her, warm and urgent. And he stayed like that, seemingly for hours, his balls tight to his body as he released, over and over again.

Sated, he lifted his weight off of her, gazing into her eyes once more and moving a lock of hair away from her face, perspiration causing it to stick to her cheek. Quietly, he eased out of her, stood and walked out of the room, returning with a wet washcloth and gently wiping her from head to toe. As their breathing returned to normal, he picked her up, cradling her to his chest and carrying her to the bed. He lay down beside her and pulled the blanket over their cooling bodies. He spoke in a soft voice, nearly whispering, "You did a great job, baby, and I'm proud of you. Always. Love you."

Chapter Four

S EVERAL WEEKS PASSED, unremarkable except for the fact that they continued to settle into the new rhythm of their life. Jordyn came into the club one night, and it turned into a double date of sorts. She sat at a table with Lucas and Vickie. Terric joined them but had to check on things periodically. A new bartender was hired on, Tristan Carraig, and he was still in training. So far, the guy seemed to be handling it fine. He was just a bit of a mystery. He didn't appear to need money, as he dumped his tips back in the communal pot when he thought no one would notice, and Terric had seen him hand the money to a homeless lady out front after work when he hadn't been able to sneak it back into the pile to be divvied up among his coworkers. Altruism was great and all, but Terric wasn't completely trusting of such gestures until he grew to know the person making them.

While she was shy at first, Jordyn soon opened up, talking to Lucas about the area and the people that had landed there to call it home. She and Vickie even acted friendly, as opposite as they appeared. Terric watched Jordyn and Lucas sitting next to each other, surprised at how easy they seemed to be in each other's company. Jordy was normally painfully shy and awkward, especially around unfamiliar males. Not tonight though. Terric wasn't picking up anything from her but relaxed enjoyment. She had a brief flash of nervousness when she first met them, but that had dispelled quickly.

They could tell she was a bit uncertain. They had put Jordy in a seat that offered her the ability to view the activity in the club, yet she was buffered from everything, with Lucas beside her and Vickie blocking the entrance to the booth. While she settled in, Lucas and Terric prevented her from feeling like the center of attention, an easy joking banter going back and forth between the two. There was a light smirk on Terric's face as he joked. "Tell me something, Lucas. Why Ascendance? Considering what kind of monsters make up the bulk of your clientele, the name comes across a bit...lofty."

Lucas hid his grin as he took a sip from his drink and set it down casually. "We picked that name because 'Demon Run Front For What We Really Do' was taken. And we heard that you should choose a name starting with A. You know, for the Yellow Pages." Jordy laughed, her face animated and her body relaxed. Terric felt a rush of gratitude. For all Lucas and Vickie liked to give him shit, they were taking care of his girl. Something about Jordyn called to one's protective instincts; not only was she a beautiful woman, she was also achingly fragile, and anyone who looked closely and had any observation skills picked up on it.

The night drew to a close, and the four of them prepared to leave. Lucas and Vickie offered to stay behind to lock up, and Terric gratefully accepted. They hugged Jordyn goodbye; Lucas kissing her cheek gently and thanking her for coming in. The two men briefly shook hands, and Vickie winked and kissed Terric quickly on the cheek, whispering in his ear before drawing back. "She's a keeper, T. Don't fuck that up." He had chuckled and entwined his fingers in Jordyn's as he walked her out of the club, lifting their linked arms in a parting wave over his shoulder.

When they were heading home, she seemed happy. Her talk was lively and manner spirited as she asked about plans for the following nights. The goal was for him to be off early on Wednesday, so they decided to make it a date night, and she quietly said she wanted to drive. Terric glanced at her, surprised, but he agreed. Then Jordyn asked him if she could have her own vehicle. She had already picked one out and wanted to go drive it the following evening, before he left for work.

Terric watched her for a moment, his expression thoughtful. "Jordyn, you do know that no one is stopping you from anything you want to do. It's up to you, baby. The only limits are the ones you choose, okay? As long as you're comfortable, that's all that matters. I'm not out to control you or to decide what you're ready for. We can go whenever you want. That's fine."

Jordyn looked at Terric and smiled softly. "I know, and I love you for it. I have a surprise for you, something I want to talk to you about, but I want to wait until we're on our date. The car is cute, so cute. It's definitely a girlie car, and you're going to hate it. But that's okay. I love it. It's red and fast and just… fun. I want to have fun.

"I'll never stop missing them, ever. I hate what my life has become though. I hate that I do this to you, make you live this life that isn't what you'd choose. And I'm sick of being scared all the time, and sad. I know I will always be sad, but I want to see if I can be something more than that, if I can be who I was before all this. Does that make sense?"

He brushed his thumb over the back of her knuckles, struck by how delicate she felt. She wasn't, though. She was growing stronger. Pride surged through him, and he grinned at her. "Yeah, it does make sense. Definitely, baby. You've been doing so well. Moving here has agreed with you. I wish we had done it sooner. I guess just a change of scenery was the key. Your car sounds great. I can't wait to see it. I bet you look hot as fuck driving it." He winked at her surprised expression and continued, his voice once more growing serious. "Jordyn, you aren't doing anything to me. This is exactly the life I would choose. I did choose it, remember?"

They arrived home. He parked the truck and stepped out to open Jordyn's door. She wrapped her arms around his neck, hugging him tightly before pulling away to stare into his eyes. "So you mean to tell me that if I didn't exist, you would be with a female? Not with a male?"

Terric pulled away from her. The subject was one they didn't broach often, for a reason. It was off limits. He glared at her for a moment and then turned to start walking, holding her hand while moving ahead of her. He released her once they were in the safety of their apartment, his voice angry still. "Fuck's sake, Jordy, Give it a rest, okay? I'm going to bed. As soon as it gets dark, we can go look at your car." He left her standing there without another word, tension thick in the air.

That evening, he kept his promise and took her to the dealership. Talk on the way was kept light, and gradually, the awkwardness dissipated. Resisting her excitement was impossible. She was out of the truck as soon as they arrived at the dealership. The salesmen eyed her appreciatively as she made a beeline for the little red sports car parked in the front of the lot. Terric glared at the men, not liking the direction of their thoughts.

One of them struck him as decent out of the bunch, and he approached that one, ignoring all the others trying to snag his attention. The man was human, but cognizant of the fact that not all the people he came in contact with were the same. Awareness passed between the two, and Terric relaxed, immediately liking the man, David. Terric explained a bit about what they were after.

Haggling or pretending to consider other vehicles was pointless. Jordyn was practically drooling over the one she came for, the ZL1. David smiled and went to grab keys and a dealer's plate, returning and offering the keys to Jordyn after the introductions were made. He turned to Terric, his brow raised. "Do you want to come along, Terric? We'll let Jordyn drive. The car's small, but we can all fit." Terric nodded and folded himself into the back, observing Jordyn as she chatted happily. She was animated, asking questions and getting familiar with the car. Carefully, she eased her foot off the brake. She popped the clutch and was anything but smooth at first, but eventually she navigated the parking lot easily before heading for the road. He was surprised to see how competently she handled the stick shift, and he realized there still many things he didn't know about her.

Terric was mostly silent on the ride, his attention on Jordyn, watching her confidence grow after a couple of miles. She turned her attention to David when they were stopped at a light, and Terric almost felt bad for the man. When she smiled at him, Terric saw the man swallow and try to maintain a professional demeanor. She tended to have that effect on people, and the fact that she appeared unaware made her even more attractive. Terric interrupted with a couple of questions to give the man a much-needed distraction.

By the time they pulled back into the dealership, David had regained his composure, and they went into his office to complete the transaction. Private discussion with Jordyn was unnecessary. She had met his eye in the rearview mirror and firmly told him she wanted it, her thoughts squealing into his brain. He had nodded imperceptibly and then grinned at her, unable to resist her enthusiasm. When the price was decided on, he hauled out his checkbook, figuring on making it quick and easy, but she had stayed his hand. She leaned up and whispered into his ear, asking if she could do it herself by making payments. Terric drew her into the hallway and asked her why, his feelings somewhat hurt that she didn't want him to purchase the little Camaro for her. She simply stared up at him, her eyes large in her face, and said she wanted to learn to be an adult for a change.

Her logic was impossible to argue with, so he nodded and replied, "Of course, Jordyn. We'll just put a down payment and let them do financing with a bank. That's fine." They walked back into David's office and told him the plan, and an hour later, Terric was following Jordyn home in her new car.

The interest rate was insane because of her lack of credit history. Terric kept her paperwork current, a must in their modern society, but he had never worried about her credit or work history; it simply hadn't occurred to him. He watched her sit in the car and glance excitedly around for a few minutes. She grabbed the owner's manual from the glove box and her paperwork before stepping out and running her fingertips along the sleek paint. She even loved the name of the color… red hot, like the candy. She approached him, stepping up on her tiptoes and kissing his mouth softly. He tasted her tears, happy ones, as she thanked him. Terric hugged her tightly for a moment then walked her up to the apartment to see her safely inside before he headed back down to his truck and left for work.

The club was hopping already when he arrived; Ladies' Night always packed a crowd. Lucas was leaving. Terric passed him on his way to the suite of offices. The two exchanged small talk, and then Lucas paused, regarding him oddly for a moment. Terric caught the sense that the other demon was trying to read him and quickly shut him out. "Man, what the fuck is your problem? You mind?"

Lucas shook his head slightly and apologized. "Listen, man, sorry. That cop, Emmett, was in today. He can… see shit. He's demon, like us, but he can see shit we can't, shit that hasn't happened yet. He is vague as hell, and most of the time you want to kick his ass for some straight answers, but he asked about you. You and your girl. I know you are private beyond anything I have ever seen before. Fuck, we've had A-list celebrities in here that are more open about shit than you are. But anyway, he wanted to know what your deal was, if she was safe. With you." Lucas held up his hand in a classic 'hold on' gesture before Terric could shred him for considering the idea that Jordyn was unsafe with him. "It was as if he thought she was in danger. He wasn't outright accusing, just… trying to feel out the situation. I know you love her. It's obvious, and she is in no way threatened by you. I told him that. I told him about you two being in here, that she was whole and hearty and all that shit, but he kept asking questions. Who else she was around, who would want to hurt her. If she worked or had friends that she hung out with. I tried to explain to him that you didn't isolate her; she was in here socializing after all, but that she seemed a bit shy. You have any light you can shed on this? Cause, man, as much as I hate to insult you, if something is wrong or something happens to her because I didn't ask, I am going to have a hard time, you know? Can't really give myself a pass because I didn't want to become involved. I hate that shit. Not only will I not forgive myself, but Vickie won't forgive me either, and rightly so. She took a liking to your girl; we both did. So trust me. I'm not asking to pry or be a dick. I just need to know."

Terric stood there for a moment, his thoughts on Jordyn and what this Emmett may have seen to put him on alert enough to go talk to Lucas about it. Finally, he answered, his voice low. "Look, man, I understand, I do. That's the only reason why we're even discussing this. It's private. And it better stay that way, got it? I appreciate the fact that you care about her, so here it is. I don't know how good your boy Emmett is, if he is confusing the timeline of what he sees. If it's the past, then that makes sense, as she was married and her life was hell. Not only was her life hell, but her marriage, her husband, took away everything that mattered to her, and she has carried that since. She blames herself. I can't really give you details, as it's her story to tell, but it was brutal, and I don't know many that would have survived what she did. Hell, I don't know that I could have survived what she went through, not with any real sanity when I came out the other side. She made it, but she's... different. She shut down, and she nearly did die. She couldn't feed. The fucker even stole that from her, basic needs. He left her unable to meet her body's basic needs in peace. She also couldn't function or feel or cry or do any of the things that let a person know they are alive. Sex was a huge issue as well, and also the key. She needs to feel pain to experience pleasure. Not just to experience pleasure, either. It's like pain unlocks everything else. And that's where I come in. I... I provide pain in a safe environment. Until she breaks. She's come a long way, and we honestly haven't really had to have any intense... sessions in a long time. She has been more aware of her needs and hasn't let it get too far, and she has also been far more independent lately. So like I said, I'm not sure what your boy is seeing, but it must have been either something from her ex or maybe from one of our past sessions. But I assure you, I provide pain, but I don't harm her. I would never truly hurt her, nothing that would cause actual physical harm to her, I'm careful. And that is as much as you are allowed into our private business. Is it enough for you to let this cop, Emmett, know he can back off? She's with me now. Nothing bad is going to happen to her. I don't let her out of my sight long enough for there to be any danger."

Lucas nodded, his expression neutral. "T, look, this guy, Emmett, he's good. Very good. If he says there's something to worry about, I would listen, okay? I'll tell him we spoke, and ask him to talk to you. He came to me first in case you were the threat, and I never thought you were, but promised to speak to you. I think maybe he should talk to her, too, if you think she would be agreeable to it. I'm going to head out, but will be happy to stop by your place tomorrow if you want, be there when he talks to her."

Terric said that was fine and turned to head to his office. He wanted to call Jordyn before the night became too busy, let her know that they would be having company. Lucas clapped him on the shoulder and headed out. He was off and had plans of his own with Vickie. When Terric unlocked his door, he dropped his keys onto his desk and picked up the receiver on his desk phone, dialing home. He received no answer, so he waited a little while and then tried again. After the third attempt, he frowned and called Jordy's cell phone. She picked up just before it went to voice mail, sounding out of breath. Alarm shot through him, making his voice harsher than intended. "Where the hell are you?"

She paused for a moment, and then her frosty reply came at him, letting him know exactly how much she did not appreciate the question. "Excuse me?"

Terric forced himself to sound calmer, and his tone softened. "Sorry, Jordyn, but I've been trying to reach you. Where are you, please? You aren't home. I can hear you're on the road, but why? What's going on? You okay?"

Jordyn still didn't sound that thrilled, but she answered him, her voice halting a bit at the end. "I'm driving yes. I wanted to go for a ride, to go see… something. I'm fine. You said I was free to come and go. Are you reneging on that? Change your mind?"

Terric bit back a sigh, trying to hide his exasperation. "No, Jordyn. Just checking. Something's come up. Lucas wants to come by tomorrow and bring a friend of his, Emmett. Apparently, the guy has a gift and sees things. I told them you were fine, safe and all, but they want to come out to check on you, I guess see for themselves. And also talk to you. It will probably be in the afternoon. That alright?"

Jordyn sounded strange, distracted, when she answered that she was fine with them coming to talk to her. He let it go and then asked her to text him when she returned home or if she needed him for any reason. Terric was unsettled by the entire conversation and urged her to be careful, and to please hurry and get home. She agreed and quickly hung up the phone.

When he went out to the bar area, Tristan Carraig was working, and for him, that meant his shirt was off and he was lying on the bar while a tourist did a body shot off his abs. Terric rolled his eyes and sat back to watch. So far, the new bartender was working out perfectly. Man-whore enough that the ladies flocked to him, yet he still put in a hard day's work.

Terric had seen him acting as his own bar back most of the time, and he didn't let long lines at his bar faze him. And shit, he was popular with the females. It had to be the dimples; the ladies ate that shit up. Terric had seen it in action. One girl would be all pissed off and ready to slap the shit out of him for flirting with another girl, and the smile would flash and all was forgiven. From what Terric could tell, he didn't have anyone in particular he dated, but several women seemed to want that honor. He shook his head as Tristan hopped off the bar, dropping the fifty into the tip jar and turning to help the next customer. The next couple hours passed quickly. A fight started just outside the VIP area, and he was there to help break it up. His bouncers were solid. They didn't need the help, but he wasn't the type to stand back and watch. He was in his office going over the inventory and preparing an order when his phone went off, a simple text from Jordyn letting him know she was home. He debated calling her and then decided not to; she seemed to need some space.

A knock sounded on his door, and he glanced up, surprised when Alyx peeked her head around the corner. He told her to come in, and she did, sitting down quietly across from him. He watched her expectantly, waiting for her to speak. As it became clear she wasn't going to, he gently asked her if she was okay. She nodded and quietly asked him if she could pick up extra shifts, maybe get promoted to assistant bar manager or something.

He frowned. Something was off in her demeanor. Normally, someone who was asking to be considered for promotion would be more earnest, but she seemed to be embarrassed and unhappy to say the least. Terric wondered if she was actually interested in a promotion or if she was doing it at someone else's prodding. He told her he would keep her in mind for the extra shifts and to talk with her co-workers if she hadn't already, and that he would get back to her on the promotion.

He watched her carefully as she gave a slight smile, thanked him, and quietly left the office. If she was in trouble or needed something, he would be glad to help her out, but if she was in actual danger, that needed to be solved. He made a couple notes for himself in his computer, sent an email off to Lucas regarding the possibility of an assistant manager position, and began to tie things up for the day.

TERRIC ARRIVED HOME less than an hour later, and Jordyn was there. She was distant and distracted. He tried talking to her, but her replies were short, and she made it obvious she had no desire to interact. They decided to stay in and spent the next couple of hours avoiding each other. Terric was reading, lying on the couch. Jordyn had been moving back and forth across the apartment for several hours, her actions appearing disjointed and purposeless. At one point, he had simply stared at her, his brow raised in a silent question. She had shaken her head in wordless denial, and he let it go. Eventually, he set his book aside, allowing his eyes to drift closed.

She came and woke him, imploring him to go to bed with her. Terric's eyes bored into hers for a moment, trying to determine the reason behind her mood change. She gave nothing away, a fact that took him by surprise. His Jordy was normally an open book. He started to question her, but broke off abruptly at her expression. She shook her head once more, quietly asked him to give her some time to think, and said she would let him know when she was ready to talk. Terric reluctantly agreed, silently grabbing a pair of underwear on his way into the bathroom to shower before going to sleep. He used the time in the bathroom to attend to hygiene needs, but also to take care of the erection that had begun when she woke him and became more persistent as she had begun to undress for sleep.

When he returned to the room, she was wearing a thin tank top, and the sheet was pulled only to her hip, revealing a mere scrap of material covering her golden skin. Terric averted his eyes and groaned inwardly. She had to know her effect on him, and he wondered if she was trying to explore a new facet of her sexuality, one previously latent. He almost hoped that were the case, as he found the idea of drawing this playful nature out of her enticing. However, it wouldn't be one he could tolerate for long, this teasing.

He stepped up to the bed to discover her sound asleep, snoring lightly. Not teasing, sleeping. He sighed and drew the sheet up higher, covering more of her mouthwatering perfection. He moved to his side of the bed, easing in, and turning away from her. Sleeping nude was far preferable, but would make it even more difficult to ignore the proximity of her body. Eventually, the even rhythm of her breathing lulled him to sleep, and he let himself drift fully into a deep slumber, something he didn't do often.

He awoke abruptly, hearing the soft snick of the front door lock. Jordyn wasn't in bed. He slammed out of the room and ran through the apartment, jerking the front door open and tearing after her. She had already reached the bottom of the stairs, and he flashed in front of her, his hand closing around her upper arm and holding her until she met his stare. "Where are you going? Why didn't you wake me, Jordy? What happened?"

Jordyn closed her eyes, unable to bear the intensity in his glare. She always felt small and insignificant, except when Terric focused that gaze on her. Then she became something more than the one who had caused so much misery to everyone. She wasn't just the idiot who made foolish choices and brought a piece of shit into her life that had caused her entire family's world to shatter.

She was torn, though. She was arriving at a point that she wanted to be able to be more on her own, without needing someone to provide that for her. Terric had done that for her, brought her to the point that she recognized that she needed to give that to herself. She just didn't know how, and it frustrated the shit out of her. His protection, once so vital to her, was starting to suffocate. Her irritation showed, and in a rare fit of temper, she lashed out at him. "I don't need your fucking permission, T. I don't. I'm not stupid, and I am not a child. I can go out when I want. And I can go out alone. I don't need a bodyguard!"

Terric dropped his hand from her arm and took a step back. His expression was furious, his tone cool. "I apologize, Jordyn. I didn't realize you had important errands to run that superseded your ability to be polite and give me the courtesy of letting me know you were leaving. For all that you say you aren't a child, you are behaving as one. You're right, of course. You are free to come and go as you please. I trust you will let me know when I am needed."

His icy glare held her for a moment longer before he turned and walked past her, continuing until he was back in the apartment. He felt her indecision as she stood, felt her eyes on him for a moment before she drew in a breath and then walked away, her determination still strong. Terric entered their home and glanced around, his face a mix of bewilderment and irritation. He walked around, straightening up stray items and then realized it was a futile gesture. Neither of them left things sitting around, he was just looking for a way to pass time.

He sank down into the recliner, his head resting on the seat back as he surveyed the place. Their home was neat, tidy. And devoid of life. If this is what she stared all those hours he was at work, he understood why she was acting irrationally. This silence of the place would drive anyone nuts. She had spent enough time in a prison of sorts, and now he may have done the same thing to her in a way. Isolated her when he had been trying to protect her. He was still going over how to fix it, his gaze straying constantly to the clock on the wall, when he heard her coming up the stairs. Less than a half hour until sunrise and she was just coming home. His jaw ached with the amount of pressure he put on it, grinding his teeth to keep from interrogating her or pointing out the time.

Jordyn walked in, dropping her keys in the bowl by the front door before glancing at Terric sitting in the chair, staring at her. Part of her wanted to go to him and beg forgiveness, but she shoved that part down, refusing to give in. It would make it that much harder to do what she needed to do. Instead she wordlessly stepped over to him and dropped a kiss on his lips before turning to head to the bedroom. He grabbed her hand, holding her for a moment before kissing her wrist lightly. She tilted her head and looked at him, the unspoken question in her eyes.

"Jordy, I'm sorry. This place… It's not good for you to be alone here all the time. I didn't realize, and I'm sorry. We can move, go back to New York, or wherever you want to go. If you like it here, we can move to a different place nearby. I just want you to be happy, baby. Tell me what you want, and we'll do it."

Jordyn's expression softened and she moved closer to him, dropping to the floor between his knees, resting her arms over his muscular thighs. Terric reached down and stroked a hand over her head, his fingers moving through her hair and against her scalp as she arched briefly into his touch. She was silent for a long time, debating. And then she knew she had to say something. She was being unfair, letting him take the blame for what was going through her head. Her voice was barely above a whisper, stress and uncertainty taking away her ability to give her words any sort of volume. He moved his head lower to hear her better. And promptly recoiled when he heard what she was saying, his mouth set in a firm line. "No."

Fire flashed in her eyes, impatience and frustration giving her courage. "Terric, I am not asking your permission. I'm telling you. I want to live alone for a while. I need to; it's time.

You can't tell me no. We aren't mated. We aren't related. We really aren't anything, are we? Freaks and misfits? That's not enough to base a fucking life on. Dammit, T. Are you hiding behind this? This noble vision you have, that you are fucking saving me? No. Not anymore. You aren't saving me now. You're making it impossible for me to get my life back because all I do is let you shield me from everything."

Terric made a move toward her, his hand reaching out to touch her, perhaps try to soothe her, and it pissed her off more. She batted him away, her expression stony, resolved. "I would rather be fucking dead. It would have been better if I had been killed when the rest of them were. At least there would have been some honor in that, dying to protect the ones I love, even if it were my fault they were in danger. Instead? I lived. I was given a second chance, and I am fucking squandering it. If I didn't deserve to live before, I definitely don't now. Yeah, T. I would rather be dead than be here with you. Not one more fucking year lost to this shit. Not one more day! Self-pity and being sheltered by some male? You think you are doing this for me? You are doing it for yourself. You're sheltering me so you have someplace to hide. You're a coward. Well, from now on, you will have to find someone else to hide behind, while you prop them up. It's time I stood on my own. I found a place. I'll be out by the end of the week."

Terric stood there, his face expressionless, except for his eyes. The pain of her words, the slap of them, was evident in the anguish in the depth of his eyes. He loved her, had always loved her. Maybe not in the traditional way, and he knew theirs was not a mated bond, but he had thought she had loved him in return, or at least had cared for him. His hand dropped to hang empty by his side, closing into a fist before he visibly forced himself to relax it. He may not recognize this version of Jordyn, but he knew she would still scare easily. Would still be intimidated by physical threat, and a closed fist is nothing if not a threat.

He nodded. His mouth opened and then closed without a word, and he turned and headed to his bedroom, not the one they usually shared. When he closed the door behind himself, he stood; leaned against it for a moment, bent over with his hands on his knees and his head hanging low. After several moments, he straightened. Being on the opposite side of the apartment wasn't far enough. He needed to leave. He was feeling suffocated, claustrophobic.

She was inhibited by the sunlight. He wasn't. He generally stayed in during the day out of consideration to her and what she was unable to do. He craved sunlight, open air, the beach. He needed the lighthouse. He opened the door and headed out, not turning his head in either direction, unwilling to face her anger or even her questions, at the moment. He grabbed his keys off the table and left, locking the door carefully behind him before taking off down the stairs and heading for his truck. The old V8 roared to life, and he headed toward the water, rolling his windows down to catch the tangy salt air as he drew nearer.

When he parked, he dragged in his first deep breath since he had woken to find her missing. He headed off toward the lighthouse, noting how few people were about at this time of year. There was a bite in the air, and he welcomed it, dropping to sit on the sand and letting the sounds of the ocean crash over him, crowding out the rest of his thoughts for the moment. He needed the distraction. If he kept playing over every piece of their life since they had moved to Province-town, trying to find that one defining moment that had been the catalyst for his entire world falling apart, he would go mad.

Chapter Five

THE STREETS WERE fairly quiet still, and it had just started to grow dark when Terric left the beach. The sunset had been spectacular, and he had largely missed it. His life had been picked apart, examined and discarded by him, and the sun's showy exit for the day hadn't roused more than a cursory notice. Terric had denied himself the sight, instead focusing on the pain and regrets he carried. He could drag himself down all he wanted, another matter completely for him to deny Jordyn the chance to flourish. He looked at his watch and debated. In the end, he decided to head to the bar, see if anyone wanted the night off.

As he drove down the streets, a light mist started, and he wondered briefly if snow was in the near future. He took a shortcut, skirting the main drag and driving along the back way. He could peer down and see the alleys between the buildings. Provincetown wasn't huge on crime, but much of it happened in these tucked away corners. He caught something going on down the alley by the club and stopped, staring out the open window of his truck.

He inhaled deeply. Human and vampire stood, facing each other. Both entirely aware of what the other was, both focused on taking what he wanted from the exchange. The human wanted money, with little concern for anything else, and he had complete disregard for the evil standing before him. He had no worry for the threat he was facing. For his part, the vampire was the same, without regard for the human life he held in his hands at that moment. Then again, he had no regard for his own life either. Terric stared a moment longer, and then apathy struck him hard. The vampire turned and met his eyes, a cold semblance of a smile crossing his features. Terric nodded once and drove off. When he pulled into the parking lot of the club, he rolled up his windows and sat for a moment, listening to the radio and staring at the phone in his hand. He wanted to call Jordyn, tell her it was okay. But that wasn't his to give her; she didn't need his blessing. She was right. Permission was no longer his to grant, only while she had given him that authority, and clearly, she had revoked it. He wouldn't impose on her will any longer.

There was a definite line between being dominant and being an overbearing asshole. He had never actually identified himself as a Dom in any way, but he recognized that he did have a dominant personality. They had fallen into a pattern over the many years they had been together, and he had stopped looking for her cues, apparently. She would always have a submissive personality, but she wanted to stand on her own. She had that right, and he wanted her to, was more proud of her now than ever. It still hurt though, and that surprised him. He wouldn't have thought it possible; he wasn't an emotional being.

The thing was, it took a lot for him to feel anything for

anyone. But when he did, he felt deeply. If someone mattered to him, they always would. Most just never arrived at that point with him. He was too adept at weeding out bullshit. Far too many people, both otherworlder and human, had hidden agendas. He had no time for that shit, and those types were cut early and completely from his life.

Jordyn, though. Jordyn had come into his life during a brutal time for her, and she had managed to slip past every barrier he had. Every protective instinct he possessed had been raised, and all he had wanted was to shield her from anything that could touch her. Never again would she be subjected to fear, pain, or sadness. The promise he had made was not just to himself, but to her as well. How would he protect her if she weren't with him? He doubted she would take well to him watching her from a distance, and stalking had never been his thing.

Terric's head lifted. Movement past his truck had caught his eye. People were arriving, starting to head into the club. He saw a richly dressed couple pull up and valet park. The blonde held out her hand, and the male reached for it, helping her out of the low-slung sports car, an American classic that even Terric had to admit was a sweet ride.

The two were regulars, doctor types that worked at Provincetown Mercy, a hospital that catered to otherworld beings. He had heard that the male owned the place but had discounted that as a rumor. No one actually owned a hospital. The two of them were unbelievable to see, both so spectacularly beautiful they didn't appear real. Most paranormal beings were above average in appearance. These two took it a step further.

Terric watched the valet eye-fuck the female, and it pissed

him off. Not nearly as much as it pissed off the male though. Dane. That was his name, he suddenly remembered. Dane and Dacia. Not sure if they were mated, but they damn sure seemed like they belonged together. Dane had turned to take in his surroundings as he moved his body behind Dacia's to head up the stairs, and as he did, he caught the valet's disrespectful gaze upon Dacia's ass. His lip curled back, revealing an impressive set of fangs. Just as Terric stepped out of his truck to save the valet's life long enough to fire him, another car pulled up—an ostentatious import—and out sprang the male from Mulligan's. Kevin.

Terric hesitated for a moment, his mind spinning, memories of that meeting and the images from his shower assaulting him. Thankfully, Kevin was distracted. He appeared to know the couple and was intent on the same thing Terric was; keeping Dane from killing the valet. Kevin met Terric's eyes for a moment and then called out to Dane; his voice friendly the first time, then low and serious when it appeared that Dane hadn't heard him.

Terric calmly walked over and grabbed the arm of the valet, jerking him to the side and blocking his line of sight to the female doctor. The nametag said Jake Sanchez. He was a shifter, a smartass and young. He started to jerk his arm away from Terric's grip with a biting reply until he took in the expression on Terric's face. He swallowed hard and then rearranged his features, his entire demeanor changing. "Hey there, boss man. Sup? Didn't expect to see you here tonight. Aren't you off? Hey, about that, before... I didn't mean to. She smelled really fuckin' good, right? Vamps aren't my thing, but damn, she's hot. Didn't catch any scent to tell me she was anyone's property, ya know? Shouldn't that mean she's free agent? Free game, whatever you want to call it. Didn't realize GQ behind her was going to get all territorial over tail he didn't have any claim to. My mistake, though. I shoulda known that nothing is normal with the vamp types."

Terric closed his eyes and dug deep for patience. The phrase 'shifter pup' kept playing over in his mind, a litany to remind him to be nice. When that didn't work, he tried to count to ten. Then again, and then on to thirty. Finally, he opened his eyes and spoke slowly, with exaggerated patience. "Isn't Tristan your cousin? He's vampire. Right? At least part? Forgive me if I'm mistaken, but I thought that you obtained the job here based on your relation to him." Terric watched the kid carefully, waiting for his nod before continuing. "So… apparently someone in your family disagrees, and 'vamps' are entirely their thing. Now, you're pretty new here and clearly not all that bright. You are here as an employee, so you aren't allowed an opinion on the various species that frequent this establishment. And whether or not he claimed her, he probably isn't all that interested in having you imagine your hands all over her. That's the thing, Jake. People come here so they can be comfortable among their own kind. Not stared at and not have their females harassed by dirt bags. You want to be a whore, that's fine. Be a whore like your cousin is, in a classy way, you know? That shit makes all of us a lot of money. No one is offended. No one is upset. Everything is fun and games with that one, you know? Hell, she's likely to be licking shots off him at some point, and everyone will laugh about how cute and harmless it is. See the difference? He will treat her with respect the entire time. And that male will let him live. Not so sure about you, though. I think you may want to make yourself scarce when they're ready to head out."

Jake merely stared at him, his face pale as he thought over the words. His parents would kill him if he lost this job. Kill him twice if he caused Tristan, the once golden one, to get fired. It sucked. None of them needed money, but still, they insisted he work. It was normally cool, gave him something to do and he loved the cars, but he truly despised being lectured. He schooled his features into a mask of deferential apology. Meanwhile he seethed inside. His voice was smooth, however, when he answered the demon staring at him as if he would like an excuse to eliminate him. "Sure thing Boss, I gotcha. Sorry, was stupid of me, won't happen again. Not to worry, we're clear. Thank you."

Terric stared at the shifter, unmoved by the little speech, but willing to let it go at the moment. He nodded and released the male's arm. The shifter stepped back, but kept his eyes firmly on Terric's. Terric turned, deliberately cutting him off, letting him know that he didn't feel it dangerous to turn his back on the young shifter, a move designed to insult and emasculate the kid.

Terric had used up his patience and was beyond the ability to feign diplomacy at that point. He stalked up the stairs, and as he passed Dane, he briefly met the vampire's stare and inclined his head to acknowledge the situation had been noted and handled. Dane returned the gesture and then turned back to his party. Kevin and Terric made eye contact for the briefest of moments, but before Kevin had a chance to speak, Terric headed to the private suite of offices, determined to lock himself away from further contact and focus on work for a few hours.

When he was seated at his desk, the scene with Jordyn

kept playing in his mind. Finally, he moved his desk phone closer, picked up the receiver, and held it in his hand. After debating for a moment, he hung it back up. Frustration had him dropping it a bit too forcefully. Terric turned on his computer and opened up his spreadsheet with the wait staff's schedule. Thirty minutes later, he realized he was still staring at the same screen. He hadn't made any changes, hadn't even begun to work on the following week's schedule. With an impatient sigh, he shut the machine off, not even bothering to power it down correctly.

Terric approached the bar, and when Tristan met his eye, he nodded. A moment later, he accepted the glass of Devil's Cut, neat. The place was filling up. It was that time of night when the crowd started to become a separate entity, taking on a life of its own. This was a critical time in any club, pack mentality being unpredictable to begin with. The intensity doubled with otherworlders. Banning them from bringing weapons was impossible; their entire body was a weapon, predators by design. The club normally stayed chill, a place to see and be seen, meet up with friends, relax, and not have to pretend as one would at a human establishment.

Theirs was the place to go when one wanted to partake in certain activities. The Trespass side of the business had been booming lately and, with that, bringing a more diverse clientele into Ascendance. Terric saw Dane and Dacia dancing, their moves flawless and graceful, yet utterly devoid of heat. No, not a couple. He wondered briefly if Dane were doing as he was, pretending. His glance grew speculative as he watched the couple more closely.

At that moment, the dance ended, and the couple went back to their table. Terric noticed then who was sitting with them. Kevin. Terric's eyes closed, and he changed the direction of his gaze; his thoughts were another matter. The image of Dane and Dacia, with their perfect looks and cool demeanor made more sense, now. Dane and Kevin. T frowned, unable to shake the image of Kevin with the handsome doctor.

Terric lifted his glass to his lips and then raised a brow. The vampire had approached, typical vampire fashion, no movement that would have been visible to a human. Although, now that Terric was close to the male, he noticed it. Not full vampire, but a hybrid wolf shifter. Terric noted that his own wolf was taking the male's measure, not completely displeased at being so close to another alpha, but not settled either. Dane seemed to be doing the same, giving his wolf time to calm before engaging Terric. Finally, a hand was extended and a friendly smile offered. They had never formally introduced themselves, so they got that out of the way, and then Dane thanked him for stepping in. Terric raised a brow, and his head tilted in an unasked question.

Dane's voice was smooth, relaxing. Terric could picture how he would be with a patient. The calming demeanor would be an asset then, likely. "Thanks for that. With the valet. I know he's a kid, and I shouldn't let that shit bother me. Hard to control it sometimes, as you know. I have other gifts at my disposal, but in the heat of the moment, instinct takes over. She may not be mine, but I'll be damned if some fucking mongrel is going to harass her."

Terric laughed and looked over his shoulder at Tristan. The vampire was standing behind him, had been as soon as Dane had approached, and Terric approved of his thought process. Have each other's backs, always. Until one knows there is no threat, there is always a threat, and remaining alert was imperative. Terric gestured to Tristan, keeping his eyes on Dane. "Your family almost diminished by one member tonight, Tris. Dane here thinks maybe your cousin is a mongrel. What do you have to say about that?"

Tristan chuckled, but the mirth didn't quite reach his eyes. He met Dane's intense stare, his voice low. "Well, yeah, that may be true. However, out of the three of us, he's the only pure anything. He is young, though. And a pain in the ass, I'll give you that. Just the same, he's family, and I won't take kindly to anyone deciding stupid is a reason to die. I'll take him in hand myself. That side of the family, it's by mating that we're related, but that doesn't make them any less family."

Terric glanced at Tristan and then again at Dane. He kept his tone light, but let it be known that Dane was not to take the issue further with the kid. It would be handled. Shit, Tristan was probably going to be much harder on the kid than Dane would. "Ok then, that's settled. He won't bother your female again, and Tristan will teach him about manners."

Dane's eyes held Tristan's for a moment longer, and then he relaxed once more. His manner was calm as he ordered an Irish whiskey on the rocks. With drink in hand, he turned to survey the crowd, the intelligence in his eyes evident as Terric watched him take in every detail. Terric told Tristan that Dane's drink was on him, and Dane nodded his thanks.

T studied the crowd himself, noticing a different feel to the atmosphere. He stood, restless, and tried to pinpoint the source. Dacia approached them then, Kevin in tow, alert and ready. Terric shook hands with Kevin, nodding as if he hadn't met the male before, and gave Dacia a gentle kiss on the cheek. She fascinated him with her quiet strength. He sensed a directness to her that many may have found uncomfortable.

Dane peered over at Kevin and asked that he take Dacia home. The two spoke quietly, and it struck Terric that they both had a hint of Ireland in their voice. Dane set his drink down on the bar and kissed Dacia's lips, more than platonic but not overly possessive, either. He and Kevin shook hands, and then Dane turned to Terric. "My brother is going to take Dacia home, but I'll hang around for a bit. Not that you need my help at all, but something is… off. I'll stick around and satisfy my curiosity if you don't mind. I don't often have this sense of foreboding. I want to make sure I'm wrong."

Terric shrugged, his attention still on the strange turn the feel of the club had taken. "Man, you are free to stay as long as you like. Excuse me for a moment, though." As Terric set his glass on the bar, he filed the information that Dane and Kevin were brothers away in the back of his mind, telling himself he didn't know why it mattered to him. He strode through the club, making his presence known, and nodded to a few regulars. The crowd parted for him, and he saw Lucas coming from the hallway where the suite of offices were, the two demons making brief eye contact before deciding wordlessly their strategy for checking out the club. Tristan came out from behind the bar, and several of the bouncers eased out of the shadows. The club goers were, by and large, unaware of any potential issue, and the goal was to keep it that way.

At the back of the club, Terric and Lucas met up, their expressions grim, focused. Terric's head whipped around, and he jerked his chin in the direction of Trespass. Lucas nodded, and the two began to make their way down the stairs, leaving Tristan at the elevator with a bouncer. At the bottom of the stairs, they heard shouting and turned in unison to investigate, both running when the tone of the argument grew more heated. As they pushed open one of the doors leading to the outside, a car pulled up and a door slammed a fraction of a second after they heard a body hit the ground. They reached the downed male at the same time, and Lucas gently rolled him over, his hands immediately going to a long wound seeping blood, applying pressure while he called out to Terric, his voice harsh with the realization the wounded was one of their own. "Valet kid, knife wound. Fuck, Terric. What's this kid's name? I don't think he's going to make it. Come over here and fucking do something!"

Terric took in the severity of the kid's injuries and yelled to Lucas that he would be back. They had a doctor upstairs. He flashed back to where Dane was and grabbed his arm, quickly explaining the situation. The two returned to Lucas, who was now trying to calm the panicked shifter and keep him in his human form. The wound was jagged, not a regular knife, so the responsible party had known they would need something more substantial to damage an immortal. Terric turned to Dane, his face deadly serious. "Doc, personal feelings aside, that's a kid, and he's one of ours. His cousin is going to fucking lose it in about five seconds, so I gotta know, because when he sees you kneeling over the kid, it's going to be all I can do to keep him off you. Will you take care of Jake? He's obnoxious but harmless, no one deserves to be gutted parking cars, at his first job."

Dane was already stripping off his jacket, rolling his sleeves up as he dropped to his knees beside the shifter. He nodded absently to Terric, already going to work. "Keep the cousin away. He doesn't need to see this, and I don't have time to fuck with him and take care of Jake."

Terric noted a calm emanating from the doctor, and he nodded with approval of Dane's use of the kid's name. He saw the doctor's lips move as he talked softly to his patient and noticed some of the tension that had twisted Jake's features ease somewhat. He turned away just in time to launch himself at Tristan, who was gearing up to take the good doctor down to the floor, his face enraged. The two began to struggle, and Terric felt the full force of that meaty fist as it slammed into his jaw. He yelled to Lucas as he once again tried to block the vampire hybrid from gaining access to the kid laid out on the floor.

Lucas had been outside, searching for any sign of who had done it, but came bounding in, fangs bared, as he gripped Tristan by the throat. The two of them together slammed the enraged bartender into the wall. Lucas was at Tristan's ear, his voice low and his words threatening.

Terric shook his head and sighed. "Lucas, man, that's his family. Ease off a bit. Listen, Tris, let the guy help him, okay? Dane's a doctor. He's going to heal Jake. He's not the one who… hurt him." Terric waited until he could see that reason had returned to the guy's eyes before he removed his weight from where he had been helping pin Tristan to the wall.

Slowly, Lucas did the same, and they released him altogether. Dane turned to the three of them, his expression stern but his demeanor calm. "You boys done? I called for pickup. He's going to come stay at my place for a few days. He's going to need surgery. He'll be fine. Probably be inpatient for about a week. You can meet us there when everything's tied up here. Tristan may come along if he wishes."

The three of them stood there, staring down at the doctor

until Tristan nodded mutely and stepped forward as the ambulance pulled up. Neither Lucas nor Terric were all that used to being told what to do, and neither knew quite how to react to it. Given the situation, it made sense, but it still rankled a bit. They waited silently until the kid was packed away in the back of the ambulance, Tristan in tow, and then glanced at each other. When the doctor was gone, that odd energy finally dissipated, and they were both frowning, unhappy with the idea that they were not immune to whatever gift the strange healer possessed. Both started to mention it and then thought better of it. Instead they ushered the rest of the guests out, closed out registers, and made sure the nightly closing procedures were taken care of before heading to Provincetown Mercy.

Jake was still in surgery, and the waiting room was filled with family. Shifters and vampires crowded into the relatively small area. Lucas and Terric made it a point to stop and talk to Jake's parents. His mother was a fiery little shifter, her eyes sharp but kind. His father was clearly high ranking in his pack, not alpha, but his bearing suggested he was among the inner circle. The worry for his son was evident in his eyes, the set of his mouth, but he kept it away from his mate, providing strength and comfort when he was in her presence. Tristan came over, and they all spoke for a few minutes, and then at a signal from his uncle, Jake's father, he drew his aunt aside and left the three of them to talk.

Lucas took the initiative, his voice low. "Mr. Sanchez, I'm sorry your son was hurt. It's not how we run our place, and we will find who did it. I'm told he will be okay. His job will be waiting for him when he's ready to come back. I run a clean place. Ascendance is a well-run establishment, and my people aren't fucked with. Ever. It won't happen again."

Jake's father stepped closer, his eyes moving back and forth between the demons. He showed not a trace of fear; for all that he was standing less than a foot away from two of the deadliest beings he would ever come in contact with. "No, it won't. My pack will be doing some searching of its own. I want to be sure that whatever bullshit you have going on in the back of your house isn't affecting my boy and the people who go to the club for a good time. Can you tell me that? Can you tell me my boy wasn't a casualty of the shady operation you run on the side?"

Terric drew up, offended. Lucas put a hand on his arm, staying his response. "I assure you, Sir. Trespass is not involved. The clientele there is too careful for this kind of thing. No, this was something different. It will be handled. Thank you for your understanding. We'll leave you all now, to your privacy. I trust that you will send word to us when there is any news. And tell Tristan that he also is to take as much time as he needs. They will both be paid, and we'll see them when they are ready." Lucas and then Terric shook the older shifter's hand and then turned and left, flashing back to the club.

Lucas turned to Terric, his eyes tired. He took in Terric's ruined clothes, and the obvious hit to the face and shook his head. "Sorry, man. You handled it well, though, not losing it with Tristan. He's a good guy, hell, even the kid is all right aside from the mouth he has on him. We'll figure this mess out. This kind of thing isn't going to happen, not here. I'll call Emmett and bring him in on this. Go home, man. Have your beautiful girl fix you up. I'll open tomorrow." He peered at his watch and gave a rueful smile. "Later today. Let me know if you want the day off. We have no plans. I can be here."

Terric stared down at the bloodstains on his clothes and sighed. After a brief debate, he decided to go home as is, no sense changing at work. He only did that when he was going to be there for a while. Bloodstained and rumpled was not the image he wanted to project. He clapped Lucas on the shoulder and the demons shook hands before Terric headed out the door and crossed the parking lot to his old truck.

Chapter Six

TERRIC PULLED UP at the apartment building, his face throbbing and exhaustion setting in. It took far more energy for him to hold back his temper and not using his powers took considerable effort. Aside from reading someone's mind, which he despised doing; he could compel them to do things. He couldn't outright force them to, couldn't make their bodies do what he wanted them to do, but he could plant the suggestions so strongly that the person didn't know that the thought hadn't been their own idea to begin with.

When he took a soul, he left the body dead, by whatever means necessary. At times he preferred the hands-on approach; sometimes using his hands was the only thing that satisfied the rage that the person engendered to cause him to take their soul. Other times, he was confronted by an evil so insidious that he couldn't stomach such close proximity; it made him physically ill. He would immolate that person, instead. Ash them where they stood, less remaining to taint the world around them.

The rare exception to the rule was when he was confronted with an evil shifter. He would never condemn the animal to that fate. Better that they die than be trapped in Hell with no escape. Even if the shifter's other forms were truly evil, and the human form didn't deserve the kindness, he usually just exterminated them, quickly, painlessly, and efficiently. The animal would not pay for the other's sins.

He was lost in his thoughts and realized he was procrastinating. He sat; banging his head lightly on the seat back, debating whether coming back to the apartment was a good idea. Finally, he grew tired of the bullshit. He had never been one to avoid conflict, and he and Jordyn had always been able to talk through shit. She had never spoken to him the way she did earlier, but they had to talk, and sooner would be better. She was likely holed up in the apartment, probably in the playroom, distraught and in pain. The image had him moving, and he rushed up the stairs, the key in his hand and the door thrust open nearly as fast as if he had flashed, which he had debated doing but hadn't.

The door flung open and hit the doorstop, bouncing back to his outstretched hand. Where he had expected to find Jordyn a weeping mess, he instead was greeted with boxes piled up and carefully labeled in her neat, feminine script. She was doing it, leaving. Terric stood there, speechless.

Jordyn came around the corner, another box in her arms. She glanced over at Terric and let the box hit the floor, immediately moving to his side. Terric simply stared at her, his expression unreadable. She moved her hands over his torso, searching for the source of the blood and not finding it. She peered at his face, wearing a puzzled expression. The concern deepened, joined by anger, when she saw the swelling and the bruise. Her touch was light, her fingers cool against his skin as she tilted his face back and forth, examining him from different angles. Finally, her gaze lifted to his eyes, and something she saw there made her drop her hand.

"Terric, I'm sorry. I'm sorry for the things I said, and I'm sorry that I feel this way, that I need to go. I would love more than anything to be okay with staying. I just… I can't do it, okay? I need to at least try. I know my way home, okay? And that won't ever change; you will always be that for me. You were my home when I lost everything. I've always been safe with you. I just…" Jordyn sighed, her head dropping as she stared at the floor, trying to find the words. "I just need to be unsafe for a little while, to prove that I can still do it, that I can be okay, even by myself. I can't let him take the rest of my life. He took everything that mattered and left me with nothing. You put the pieces back together, made me nearly whole again. I just need to know, for myself, if there is anything else out there for me. I want to know that I can still function, and I want to know who I am now. You held the pieces together long enough, T. It's time I tried for a while. You are home, though, and whenever I need to feel safe, hell, whenever I need to just… feel, I know my way back." Jordyn stood there, her blue eyes swimming in unshed tears, her hair in a straight ponytail cascading down her back, wearing simple black yoga pants and a mauve sweater. He couldn't decide if she resembled a co-ed or a career woman, but one thing she did not appear was incapable.

Terric stared at her, his frown in place but easing, and without a word, he leaned down and enfolded her in his arms, holding her tightly for a moment. He felt her shoulders shake as her tears won and she cried, her arms going around his neck to cling to him. After a few minutes, he drew back, staring down into her eyes and reaching out, wiping her tears. He caught one on his thumb and studied it for a minute, watching the prism dance inside the liquid as it caught the light. He rubbed his thumb along his forefinger, destroying the tear. "That's enough, Jordy. No more crying, okay? It's not up to me to decide when you're ready, but for what it's worth, I understand the need to try. You're right. You should do this. You're going to be fine. I was being stupid and overbearing, overprotective. I'm sorry, Jordyn. I'll support whatever decision you make. I want you here with me where I know you are safe. That's my problem, not yours. Just as long as you know to come to me when you need anything." Terric stopped there, realizing he was rambling.

There wasn't anything left to say and still far too much to be said. The idea of Jordyn alone was a ball of ice in the pit of his stomach. Dread filled him, and he was nearly over-whelmed with the thought of locking her up where she would be safe forever. He couldn't do that to her though; she would hate him eventually. What would start out as a safe place for her would become a cage, their home would become her prison. He shook his head to clear the dark thoughts and forced a small smile. "What do you still have left to do?"

Jordyn raised her gaze to him, love shining in her eyes. Terric was, in so many ways, the ideal man. For someone else, someday. For now, he was her savior, her best friend, and for this last night, her lover. She moved closer to him, laying her palm along the side of his face and staring into his eyes. He saw so much and could read people far too well. Yet he couldn't see himself clearly at all. She wondered who he would eventually end up with for a mate. He was surly and downright mean at times. He was unfriendly at best. Even with her, he didn't talk much. Tonight was the most communicating they had ever done, with words, anyway. But when he loved, he did it with his entire being. It transformed him, and the thought of him alone with no one to give that side of himself to broke Jordyn's heart.

She glanced toward the window. The sky would be growing light soon. Her other palm went to his face, and she held him bracketed between her hands, losing herself in his eyes for several moments. Finally, she went up on tiptoe and kissed his lips sweetly. Her voice was nearly shy as she spoke in a whisper. "Come lie with me, Terric. Make love to me and hold me. Let me touch you and feel you inside me. I want the day to sleep with you. I want it to be just us acting like a normal couple. Nothing more than two people enjoying each other."

Terric's eyes were intense, boring into Jordyn's for the length of several heartbeats before he nodded. He needed it also, needed to be inside her, to touch her and lose himself in their illusion one last time. His hands reached down, palming her ass as he lifted her, grinding against her as she wrapped those long legs around his lean waist. Her core was hot against him. He could feel the heat through the denim of his jeans, and he growled deep in his chest as his mouth captured hers. Their tongues danced together, and he carried her, wrapped around him, into the bedroom.

Terric kicked the door closed and held her against the wall, her graceful fingers working the buttons of his shirt. Jordyn pulled back for a moment and then gently kissed the bruise on his jaw, being tender with the swollen area. Her palms flattened on his chest briefly then moved over his pectoral muscles as she eased she shirt off his body. She delighted in the hard muscles under her hands, her thumbs moving over his nipples as she leaned forward and bit his throat lightly. Terric's head kicked back, and he moaned, demanding that she drink. When she didn't immediately comply, he lowered his head and stared at her, his voice more demanding.

"Jordyn, I want you to take from me, now. Like this. Show me how healthy you are, baby. How ready you are to be on your own, that you can feed in the regular way. Besides, I want the pain. I want to feel those perfect little fangs pierce my flesh. Do it. Now."

His eyes held hers for a moment longer and then slowly closed as she licked her lips, already anticipating his taste on her tongue. Jordyn threaded one hand into his hair, easing his head to the side to expose his throat for easier access. Her hand continued to dance over the planes of his chest, and she struck, relentlessly hard, letting his blood flow over her tongue. Her lips closed over the flesh, and she began to draw deeply, the suckling causing Terric's dick to harden, and she could feel it twitch against her core.

Terric caressed her ass, rolling his hips against her body while she fed. When she pulled back, her eyelids were heavy, and she had that sated and tired gaze that she often wore after feeding. Terric laughed softly, his hand cupping her cheek and his thumb making a lazy motion across her full lips. "Nope, not yet, sleepy girl. Nowhere near done with you yet."

TERRIC LAID JORDYN down on the bed gently, her hair fanned out over the pillow. The bright gold color stood vividly against the deep blue of the sheets. A small smile played across her face as she watched him move. He was so beautiful to watch, the grace that was innate to his movements was at odds with his size. He lay down beside her, and Jordyn turned to him, greedy for his touch. She rolled over, lying on her belly and reaching for the snap of his jeans. Terric propped an arm under his head, watching her movements with interest. Her breath was hot on his abs, making them tighten while she lowered the zipper. He raised himself off the bed so she could work the denim over his hips and ease it down his body, the black boxer briefs down with them. She sat up, pulling the jeans off his body, and stared down at him appreciatively.

Terric was unembarrassed, lying naked under her gaze, his cock still hard from earlier. She stroked his body with the flat of her palm, his warm, soft skin a perfect contrast to the hard muscles underneath. Her mouth closed over his cock, his back arched and his fist closed around locks of her hair. He was close. The tension between them and the shit at the club had made him edgy. Sex was the perfect way to ease the tension. Release calmed him like nothing else. Jordyn could feel the orgasm building inside Terric and stepped up her efforts, stopping for a moment to urge him to come before she took him deep into her throat. He shouted her name, and then he began to orgasm, her throat working to swallow his seed as her cheeks hollowed while she sucked him, tiny moans coming from the back of her throat.

Momentarily spent, he pulled her off him and dragged her up his body. Then his mouth slanted over hers, his tongue stroking her bottom lip, and she opened for him, their tongues exploring each other's mouths. Terric told Jordyn to undress, and she stood, her eyes focused on his as she disrobed. Her breasts were high and full, her stomach flat and her waist was small, her curves giving her the natural hourglass shape that he loved. She wasn't scrawny. Her body was lean but healthy. Terric stared at her appreciatively. Then he sat up, his hand going between her legs, and he began to slide his finger along her core, enjoying the feel of her. His eyes were hot on hers, and his voice was low. "You did great, baby, fed with no problems, and now look at this. You're wet, Jordy. Does this feel good? You made me feel so good when you went down on me; I need to show you how good. Do you like my hands on you? Like my finger sliding along this pretty little slit before it enters your tight body?"

Her only reply was a nod; speech had left her. Terric slid a second digit into her, slowly fucking in and out of her while his thumb applied pressure to her clit.

"I need to hear your answer, baby girl. You are so wet for me now, so hot. But I want to hear you say it. Tell me what you want, baby."

Jordyn blushed, her need growing. She gripped his shoulders, hard, and began to ride his fingers, her mouth open as she began to pant. Seeing how close she was, he backed off slightly. Jordyn tried to speak, but her voice broke on a sob. Finally, she managed to find the words. "You, I want you inside me, T. God, please, now."

Terric withdrew his fingers, and his hand wrapped around her wrist, tugging her to him. Jordyn's legs parted, and she straddled him. His hands gripped her waist hard, and he pulled her down on his cock, sharply entering her in one smooth thrust. She immediately began to orgasm, her walls spasming around him, and she grew even tighter. Terric called on all his control, growling low in his chest while she exploded around him. His fingers gripped her hard, and he rolled his hips under her, driving her orgasm higher.

When she began to orgasm a second time, he drove into her, his back arching as he lifted her up off the bed. Jordyn's scream tore through him as she began to milk him violently. He held her steady, and his own climax began, refusing to be put off any longer. He felt it start in his toes, his leg muscles tightening, all the way up his body, the nerves in his lower back firing signals to the rest of his body. His balls drew up tight. Her name left his lips in a hoarse cry as he began to empty inside her, filling her completely, causing her orgasm to continue relentlessly, and she rode crest after crest with him.

They lay there, panting, bodies covered in a light sheen of sweat. Jordyn had collapsed on top of Terric, and he moved the tangled mass of golden hair away from her face, holding it off her body so she cooled down. After several moments, she moved to ease off him, and he groaned softly. Jordyn sat up and smiled down at him, her expression clear and unguarded in a way he hadn't seen before. Her fingers were gentle as she once again touched the nearly faded bruises, probing the swollen area with a cool touch. She tilted her head inquisitively and stared down at him. "Won't you tell me what happened?"

Terric shrugged and gave her a short run down of his day. Truthfully, they had no idea who had gutted one of their own, but he intended to find out. His mind briefly flashed to the kid he busted, Devon. It would be worth it to see if he and Jake knew each other. Terric smiled and shook his head. First time he came home from the new job with a mark on him and from one of his own people no less, a ham-fisted bartender with a hot temper and fierce sense of loyalty. Things could be worse.

They talked for several hours, about everything and nothing. They lay together, focused on each other. They made love several more times, revisiting all their favorite positions. And then they spent a couple hours in their playroom, not for any other reason than sheer enjoyment of each other's bodies, testing limits and pushing past them. Toward the late afternoon, Jordyn fed again. That was the one thing that Terric found nearly impossible to accept, that she would be okay with feeding. He couldn't secure her promise to come to him for that though. She wanted complete independence. He promised not to walk around in her head; she promised to check in once in a while.

It was almost fully dark. They were just stalling now, and he knew it. They both did. He could tell by Jordyn's expression that she felt completely torn, and he knew he was causing that. Finally, he lifted their joined hands. Their fingers had been entwined for hours, as if both were afraid to be the one to sever the connection. Jordy out of fear of hurting Terric, and Terric because the thought of her out in the world unprotected made it difficult for him to breathe.

Terric studied their two hands, so different. They were entirely different creatures, although both had adapted to life among humans and could hide their true nature most of the time. Still, the differences between their hands were stark. His were rough, scarred. Her skin was golden, soft and supple, and her fingers were long, tapered and feminine. They were capable hands though, and he had neglected to give her credit for that for so long.

Terric closed his eyes for a long moment, offering up a silent plea to whoever would deign to listen to anything he would request that she be safe, always safe, and that her life would become what it should have been all along; happy, full. She had earned the right to feel peace and contentment. He kissed the back of her hand, rubbing his face along the impossibly soft skin. When he opened his eyes, she was watching him with tear-filled eyes.

He chuckled softly, unwilling to burden her with his sadness. "Baby, come now. It's time. We could go like this for days, and before you know it, a week has passed. Two, and then a month. Suddenly, it's been another fifteen years, and you glare at me with hatred, realizing I selfishly kept you too busy in bed to remember you had other things to do. You do, you know. You have really amazing things to go do, and you can't do them here. This place, me, us… all of this will become a cage for you eventually. It already has. I just didn't see it. Maybe I didn't want to. I've already made you promise that you'll remember your way home. And you know all you have to do is say the word and I will go to the ends of the earth to give you whatever you need."

Jordyn stood and smiled softly down at Terric as she reached her hand down and pretended to tug him up to stand beside her. They hugged silently and then headed out to the main part of the house. Her glance touched down on the collection of boxes, debating. After a moment, she turned to Terric, the sadness in her eyes somehow less haunted already. Her voice became nearly excited and she nodded once to herself before speaking. "You know what? I'm not taking this stuff with me. I have the essentials in my car. I don't want anything other than what I can pack in my car and move in one trip. I need to start building a new life, with new memories. I've been hauling around the past for long enough. It's so heavy. I just can't do it anymore. When I had you to help me carry it, that was different, but now? I think it's time I travel light for a while. I think I'll add things as I become stronger, and they will be things that have meaning to me, the new me." She paused, trying to find a way to tell him what she wanted. "Terric, do me a favor?"

Terric watched her, his eyes wary. He waited silently for her to continue. When she spoke again, her voice was husky and she spoke to him apologetically. "Stay up here. Don't walk me down. I want to walk out of here on my own with no hand to hold. If I can't make it down to my car and take myself to my new place, I need to find that out on my own. And I don't want to have an audience if I fall apart, okay? I'll text you, when I arrive at my new place. Home. I'll text you when I arrive home." The word made her smile; she was doing it, making it real, all on her own. She looked to Terric to see his reaction but he merely nodded his acceptance.

Jordyn crossed to him, her arms looping around his neck and she stood on her tiptoes to press a kiss to his lips. Terric's arms wrapped around her, pulling her into his warm embrace once again. She found herself tempted to lose herself there, and when she realized how reluctant she was to leave, she forced herself to pull back. The time had come. She kissed his cheek, her voice almost shy when she said goodbye one last time. "I won't forget my way home, I promise, T."

Terric caught her face between his palms, his eyes boring into her. "I love you, Jordyn. Always."

Jordyn's eyes were swimming in tears she tried to keep from spilling over and she turned her face, pressing a kiss into his palm before whispering in return. "Always." She drew in a shuddering breath and then stepped back, and her eyes stayed locked on Terric's as he dropped his hands to hang uselessly at his sides, unable to hide the wrecked expression on his face. He didn't try to stop her though, merely watched as she turned and slipped out the front door, closing it softly behind her.

HOURS PASSED, AND Terric stood unmoving. He replayed each day of their lives together, holding, examining and then tucking away each moment. She was the only woman he had ever deeply loved. The days ahead, without the softness she brought to his life, promised to be more than bleak. They seemed like a damned travesty. What made it even harder to accept was knowing the fault was his own, his own deficiency. With Jordyn, the world had been brighter. She had created lightness within him. She was gone, and he was alone in the dark.

Terric finally made his way out of the apartment, needing to be away from the confining walls that mocked him. He walked, endlessly. Every once in a while, he would take out his phone and read her text. Three simple words that summed up so much more than the arrival at her new place. She had simply texted, "I made it."

Pride bloomed inside him as he stared at the words once more, and thought about how far she had come. Yes. His girl had, indeed, made it. She had been through hell and had come out on the other side, not many could say that. He glanced up, realizing where he was. He had come to the lighthouse, and he watched as the beacon swept out across the water, piercing the blackness with its relentless light. He lowered himself onto the damp sand, the tang of the salt teasing his nose, and his sensitive ears picked up the sound of the wind moving through the sea grass on the dunes not far away.

Chapter Seven

T RISTAN PASSED BY Terric on his way to the club for his
first night back since Jake had been hurt. At first, the
family had tolerated the vampire's presence, but that hadn't
lasted too long. He didn't really blame any of them, and he
certainly wasn't surprised by it. Everything about him was a
constant reminder of what had been lost. Not what, who.
Seren, his baby sister, and, as she had aptly been named, her
brightness had rivaled any star. She didn't merely exist; she
had shined. And like many things that shine, the darkness that
remained when that light burned out was more than some can
handle. Many families didn't survive such a tragedy. Tristan's
family did, simply because they were able to come together in
a common purpose. They were able to bond over their hatred
of him and their certainty that he was solely to blame for the
loss that had rocked them all.

Tristan nodded at Terric, hoping for reassurance that he
harbored no hard feelings. Terric hadn't seemed to notice
Tristan. At the moment they drew abreast of each other,
Terric offered the barest flicker of recognition. Tristan tapped

on the brakes, trying to see if the male wanted to talk face to face and would be turning the truck around. The truck didn't slow.

Anger flashed briefly in Tristan's eyes; the familiar feeling of rejection was not unusual, but still a surprise coming from that quarter. The two had been on good terms, on the way to becoming friends even, he had thought. Tristan shoved the errant thought away, a mask of indifference settling over his handsome features. He swung around back to the employee parking area, pulling into his usual spot and killing the ignition. The radio stayed on, and he listened to the lyrics for a while. His head hit the headrest and he closed his eyes.

Tristan tried to remember every detail of her face, a ritual he did at least once a day. He knew it was imperative that he never forget her. He picked through his memories, settling on one of a family vacation. Their parents had been preparing to go out. Seren had been trailing around after their mother, trying to manipulate them into taking her with them. When that didn't work, she had decided to be as much of a pest as possible. She had come downstairs as they were heading for the door, face made up like a clown and shuffling forward in a pair of high heels. Miraculously, she hadn't broken her neck on the stairs. Their father had given him a stern glare. Tristan should have kept her occupied so they could leave, and now the six year old would be inconsolable.

Tristan had rushed forward, scooping her up while they dashed out the door, but he was too late. She had been crying loudly as the door shut, and the night would be ruined for their mother. Tristan sighed and then set his baby sister down, frustrated because he couldn't go out with his friends. Now, he would likely be grounded for the following night, two nights stuck at home. Great. He scowled for a moment but forced himself not to voice the thought, or complain out loud.

She calmed eventually, after several forbidden cookies. Ice cream had factored in, but mainly, having Tristan's full attention had done the trick. She had turned to him, kissing his cheek and her little girl voice had said so sweetly, "I love you, Trissy."

He hadn't cringed at the nickname for once. He was too glad she was smiling again. He had kissed her nose and replied, "I love you, too, Starry." She had giggled at his new name for her and then asked for a story.

Tristan opened his eyes, relieved, as the song ended. Something about angels and it mentioned a brother's love. The entire song could have been written for the two of them. She had definitely left too soon. Jesus, he missed her. The pain gripped him so hard that it became physical. He cleared his throat, trying to stop the tears that were threatening to fall. He glanced at the time, glad he had to get to work.

Tristan nodded to people on his way through the club. To anyone watching him, he would have appeared to have life by the ass. He was ruggedly good-looking; his eyes were nearly onyx colored, and almost always devoid of any strong emotion. They had been that way for years, empty. He was of average height, for a vampire, at a shade over six feet and four inches. His chest was broad; he had always enjoyed working out.

Nowadays, it seemed more like he was punishing his body than exercising. He was growing worse as time passed, even he knew that. A person could spend so much time waiting, hoping. He was just about at the end of that ride, and truthfully, he was grateful. When hope left completely, maybe he could move on with the business of dying. He was nearly ready. The endless parade of whores, the drinking, all of it. He was beyond exhausted. He was tired of himself.

Immortality aside, simply putting one foot in front of the other grew difficult at times. Unbearable, the thought of the next several centuries trapped in this same body, knowing that he meant little to nothing to those around him, and worse, that everyone who had the misfortune of being related to him despised him. Rightly so, still, the pain was enough to bring the strongest to their knees. He was weary, tired of fighting, and his strength had been flagging for years.

Willow stepped from behind the bar, a ready smile and a quick hug waiting for him as he approached. She embraced him, and warmth suffused him at the simple contact. He could fuck all the whores he wanted, it changed nothing for him. This was what he craved, simple caring. She was one of the exceptions. She didn't want to have sex with him, didn't want anything from him at all. She just happened to care. Pathetic, really, how much he needed that.

Willow was one of his few friends, and one of the reasons he hadn't taken off yet. She knew though, that one of these days he would be gone, likely without a goodbye. He had come to Ptown looking for something, and what he was seeking wasn't there. It likely didn't exist for him at all. Still, she made his time there more enjoyable. He picked her up off the floor and swung her around, smiling at her squeal of laughter. She was a good girl.

Tristan set her feet on the floor once again, gently kissing her cheek and asked her what she wanted done to set up for the night ahead. Willow smiled up at him, and asked him to play bar-back, stocking the main bar as well as his bar, the smaller one in the VIP area, with whatever they needed to make it through another busy night. He gave her a mock salute and headed for the storeroom to grab the two wheeled truck and load up on the basics. He would make a list when he finished with items he knew without inventorying that they would need to see them through the night.

His phone went off later in the evening. Willow was inundated with human women home from college. Her bar was packed, but she was tired of the "spoiled bitches" as she put it. She wanted a break, asked that he change bars with her, and let her run the VIP bar for a while. It mattered little to him, and he backed up all his regulars before ambling over.

Willow was well liked by the VIP crowd, and she was their regular bartender. They would be glad to see her pretty face. She thanked him as she ducked out from behind the bar, all but running to the other room. Tristan surveyed his new customers, sighing as he systematically labeled them according to stereotype. Among which was the usual assortment of daddy's girls, princesses, bitches, emo wanna-be's, goth hotties, preps and the athletic looking ones that were generally the type he favored. These ones were forsaking all the months they had spent conditioning their bodies and were pumping themselves full of alcohol. It seemed visiting the folks was stressful for these females.

Tristan started at one end of the bar and began to work his way across, trademark dimpled grin flashing, yet never reaching his eyes. He lost count of the amount of times he laid down on the bar or spread his legs for the females to do the various body shots he was famous for. The shots were a diversion, a money maker, and doing them made the night pass. For all the hands that grabbed at him, not one of them truly touched him or made any kind of lasting impression. A sad commentary, both on who he was and who they were. Truthfully, he rarely even bothered to make eye contact with any of them.

Terric entered the club toward the end of the night. Tristan watched him, his eyes tracking the demon as he made his way to the bar. The two nodded at each other as Tristan noted the tense set of the demon's shoulders, the grim set to his mouth. Tristan made his way over, dropping a coaster on the gleaming wood of the bar, unsure if Terric was working or if this was a social visit. The expression on the man's face gave him nothing to go on. Terric eyed the coaster for a moment, and then shrugged and pulled out a barstool and sat, his expression vaguely lost. Tristan turned, grabbed the bottle of Devil's Cut, poured it the way Terric drank it; neat, and set it down in front of his boss. Terric picked up the glass, finished in one swallow and then stared at the empty glass in his hand, as if surprised to see it there.

Tristan poured another. It was unusual to see his boss in anything but complete control. Finally, Terric lifted his eyes, meeting Tristan's stare squarely. The pain and the bewilderment that Tristan saw there had him seriously worried. When Willow headed over for last call a few moments later, Tristan came around the bar and approached Terric. His voice was pitched low, too low for the milling humans to hear. He urged Terric to his feet and the two made their way toward the VIP section.

Tristan slowed as they reached Terric's office, setting a glass and the bottle of bourbon he had palmed from the bar on the demon's desk. Terric nodded, his bleary gaze lifting for a moment. He uttered two words, nothing more. "She's gone." Tristan nodded, further explanation wasn't needed. He didn't know Terric's female well, but he had seen them together a few times. She had been stunningly gorgeous, and from appearances, they had been happy, and it hadn't been that long since they were last in.

That was life, though. Everything was fine and then life would come up and knock him flat on his ass, just 'cause it could. What was the expression? *What a difference a day makes.* Yeah, that was it. And then the rest of one's existence is spent waiting for another life changing day, something to set one on an even keel once again. Didn't seem to work that way though. Not that he had seen, anyway.

Balance was a great concept but elusive as fuck. Nature abhors a vacuum, Newton's laws, karma, reaping what you sow. Bullshit. All of it. Sure, the physics ones were proven and all that, but still, that only applied in the physical sense of the word, because truly, unless it stemmed from some previous existence, karma had absolutely no reason to have such a grudge against him. Nothing he had done could justify the fact that he had garnered the hatred of just about everyone he had ever loved. Not back when it all started, at any rate. And nothing that could explain the loss of Seren.

Tristan shook his head as if to dispel such thoughts. Terric had been dumped. No one was dead. No one was missing. Families wouldn't spend days searching in frigid temperatures, afraid to hope but unable not to. No, as painful as this must be for the shifter demon, getting one's heart broken by a woman was a part of life. Still, he found it hard to see the male looking so... fragmented was the only word that came to mind. Stunned, bewildered. And yeah, maybe a bit wrecked. Like he didn't know where to settle his eyes, where he could hide.

Tristan turned and clasped Terric's shoulder, mumbled a gruff apology, and then headed out to finish the closing up procedures. The laws in their small town were strict when it came time to closing down the bars and clubs. Theirs was a great little town, and the townspeople loved the fact that the otherworlders had settled in and stayed, built a life among them. That in no way meant they were exempt from the laws put in place to keep the peace.

Favoritism didn't exist when it came to that. The area was beautiful, with something to offer just about everyone. The community itself was known for its tolerance. Long before homosexuality was at all accepted, Provincetown had held parades, and was known for its welcoming attitude. Not just a tourist area, it was also an artist community. Many of the people were activists, concerned with issues that involved wildlife, conservation and marine life. People there tended to have a broader worldview. Among other things found were occult shops, head shops, tourist traps and art studios. The lighthouse called to many, its beacon guiding folks back to the small confines of a town where they knew they would be accepted.

Tristan enjoyed the same acceptance as the rest of the so-called "others," in the broad sense. He was accepted for his differences. In this town, he was as much as an anomaly as the other paranormal beings, and so he was part of that illustrious group. Within that smaller community, no. Not really. No one likes a fuck up, and he had, indeed, fucked up. His family was well known, and well liked. His immediate family as well as extended family. So when the tragedy had happened, there had been an outpouring of support and that also provided an audience for Tristan's shortcomings.

The young were revered. The children of immortals, no matter the species, were both special and rare. They were guarded and cared for and watched, not just by their own family, but by others as well. Anyone that brought harm to one would generally end up dead. Either by a tribunal or at the hands of the family, or, barring that, would just disappear one day. Some things just weren't done; every set of people had their code of conduct, so to speak, and set of ethics and mores that were inviolable. And in this, Tristan didn't really fit in any category.

There had been talk of his destruction. Those who had lost children, and knew the pain and depth of the tragedy, many of them called for him to be killed immediately. Still others wanted a trial of sorts, they wanted him to be arrested and detained by the police force made up of their kind, for the hybrid to be held in their special prison until a decision had been reached. Voices were raised, as the discussion grew heated. His family had remained silent. Jake had exploded in anger, but he had been young and his voice easily ignored. Tristan's eyes had remained downcast, and he had withdrawn into himself, not participating in the discussion of his future. He had simply been unable to think beyond the pain, and hadn't been able to summon the ability to care what happened. Had the decision been made to destroy him, he wouldn't have fought.

Tris moved on autopilot. His mind was trapped back in the past. As he restocked the bar, he moved efficiently, his hands automatically completing the tasks that he had done countless nights. He looked down at them. Closed them in large fists. The gesture was empty. It had been years since he had been able to feel strong emotion. He dropped his hands to his sides, surveyed his bar to see what else needed to be done. A credit card slip lay on the polished mahogany surface and he picked it up, noting the tip amount on it. It didn't matter. He dropped it in the register and closed the drawer without removing the cash from the till. He finished the physical part of closing, and returned to the cash register. The register beeped and gave a half ring as he took the till out and grabbed one of the canvas pouches, dumping the cash and credit slips into it and zipping it up. He tucked the pouch under his arm and grabbed a beer for himself as he headed toward the offices once more.

He glanced into Terric's office. The man hadn't moved. His eyes were sightlessly staring ahead, but they were red. Clearly, he had moved enough to polish off a good portion of the alcohol, and as Tristan watched, a tear snaked down his cheek, unchecked and apparently unnoticed. Tristan continued on, leaving Terric to grieve in private, and went to drop his money into the safe.

When he passed back through, he glanced in at his boss once more. Terric didn't turn toward him, so Tristan was able to observe him unnoticed for a few moments. Even though they had been working together for a while, he didn't feel as if he knew Terric all that well, as if the man kept himself separate from the others, more than just boss/employee distance. Tristan considered, for a minute, what the reasons behind that might possibly be. His guess was something to do with who or what he was, the demon side of things, something Tristan didn't have to deal with.

Being vampire and shifter was a pain in the ass at times. He would have preferred to be all shifter, but at least he had the freedom to move about in the daylight and he only had to feed on blood every so often. Still, on his best day, he wouldn't go through what Terric, or any other demon, had to endure. Terric must have picked up on the gist of Tristan's thoughts; he turned and eyed the bartender. Terric's expression was bleak, a bit embarrassed, and then the mask went down. His voice was derisive and held a hint of challenge. "Something on your mind, I see. You don't know a fucking thing, and unless you want me to give you a firsthand taste of what demons 'endure,' you'll drop that line of thought."

Tristan held up his hand, palm facing the demon in a classic 'hold on' gesture. "Man, just stopping to see if you need a ride. That's all. You seem like you could use..." He almost said "a friend" but something stopped him. "A ride. You're drunk. Not everyone is indestructible. Let me drive you home."

Terric closed his mouth, and appeared to think for a moment before lurching to his feet. Tristan dipped forward as if to catch Terric, when it appeared as if Terric was going to face plant. The demon stopped himself, straightening and giving Tristan a bleary grin. "I got this, man! I'm fine. Thanks, though. You're a good friend. A good, good friend..."

Tristan glanced over as Terric trailed off, waiting to see if he was done. It appeared the demon had lost his train of thought and was eyeing the bottle once again, as if contemplating another drink. Tristan grabbed his bicep and dragged him away from the desk, exhaling a sigh of relief when an arm was slung around his shoulders companionably and they began to make their way to the door.

He asked for Terric's keys, not trusting the demon's ability to hang on to the back of Tristan's motorcycle. Terric's face went blank and then he told Tristan he couldn't remember where he left them. Usually they were in his front pocket but his front pockets were at home. Tristan stared at Terric, confused as all hell. Terric appeared even more befuddled than Tristan felt, and finally, Tristan looked down at the jeans Terric wore. He nodded at them and asked if those were the pants Terric referred to. Terric nodded sadly, and said he couldn't believe he had gone out without pants.

Tristan started to laugh and then quickly hid it. Drunk off his ass or not, the demon was not one to fuck with. Finally, he gave up and simply reached down into Terric's pants pocket. He fished around for a moment, finally dragging out the keys. Terric's head whipped toward him and he drunkenly stumbled back, anger marring his features. Tristan held the keys up to show Terric what he had been doing, trying to explain as quickly as possible. "Dude, just needed your keys, swear. Don't freak on me, okay? You seemed a bit out of it and we need to take you home. Just wanted to grab the keys, I didn't touch nothing else, wasn't trying to. Fuck, man. You think that of me?"

Terric sneered, his words slurred and defensive. "You think that of me? Is that what you're trying to say? You think I'm some sort of pervert, that I want you to touch me? Or that I'm hitting on you? Don't flatter yourself. Vampires don't do it for me. Neither do pretty boys with dimples. Or people who let little girls die on their watch. Fuck you, Carraig. Nothing about you interests me."

Tristan froze. Rage filled his handsome face, and he stepped back, letting the keys fall on the floor. His hands bunched into fists and he felt his heart rate accelerate. His head began to pound and all he could do was stare. He could see the scene play out, reflected in the apathy staring back at him in the demon's eyes. This was how he could finish all of it in that exact moment. Terric was showing him how it would end, if he pushed any further. Question was, did he want to?

And yeah, he did. Not out of anger at the comments that fell drunkenly from Terric's lips. More for the possibility of escaping the relentless fucking pain. He took a step forward, the images vividly real in his mind. His death would be fucking beautiful and it would be permanent. He nodded; his eyes shining with unshed tears. "God, yes. Please, Terric. I don't care how or why, just make it fucking end."

Terric nodded, his eyes glowing red and he took a step forward, knowing he would pay for this nearly as much as Tristan. More, actually, he would genuinely wish for death when called to answer for killing a sentient being that didn't deserve to die. He raised his hand, focus etched into the planes of his face, tension changing his posture. Before he could strike, however, the path was blocked.

Emmett stood in Tristan's place. His hand wrapped around Terric's throat, rapidly cutting off his air. Terric's eyes went flat, then the red deepened, and the two began to struggle. Tristan had been shoved to the side and stood silently, watching the pair. He knew far more was going on beyond what he could see or sense. The struggle was nearly palpable, muscles were straining, he could see the tendons in Emmett's neck stand out as he strained to maintain his grip on Terric, and Terric's face was red from the exertion of trying to drag air into his lungs. That was nothing compared to the waves of psychic energy bouncing back and forth between the two, however. It gave Tristan a headache, so he could only imagine what it felt like to those two.

Emmett clamped down on his anger, keeping the task at hand impersonal. Well, as much as he could. It pissed him off to see Terric wasting his gifts, and even though time was an unlimited resource for the likes of them, he hated that the shifter demon was wasting time pretending to be something he wasn't. It disgusted him that Terric was so scared to be who he was.

What difference did it make what gender the man preferred? What had he gained by denying who he was for all these years... He wasn't straight and no one fucking cared. He was intent on living the life of some martyr, and Emmett couldn't fathom why. He enjoyed men as well as women. As long as everyone involved was happy, who cared? They were fucking demons, even just half in Terric's case, and that was far more of a stigma, if they were talking about things society didn't readily accept. Emmett was trying to delve deeper into Terric's mind, but he wasn't able to push past the blocks Terric kept in place. Terric, being a hybrid, wasn't as strong as a pure demon, such as Emmett, but he was not without defenses.

They were rapidly approaching a stalemate. Emmett couldn't really kill Terric without more of a reason than he currently had. He hadn't killed the vampire, so no parity needed to be restored. And, mercy killings, such as it would be billed as if he were to kill a being that wanted to die, weren't thought upon favorably. So they were all screwed. Tristan and Terric could court death all they wanted. It wasn't any of theirs to grant.

He dropped his hand from Terric's throat, stepping in close and speaking in low tones directly into the man's ear. Terric nodded once and began to try to drag air into his lungs, bending at the waist and propping his hands on his knees, waiting for the dizziness to pass. After giving a couple of painful coughs, he straightened and his gaze locked on Emmett, their eyes meeting as an understanding was reached.

Terric approached Tristan, his face solemn. He stuck out his hand, trying to ignore the curiosity on the vampire's face. Tristan didn't extend his hand, just continued to glance from Terric to Emmett. Finally, Terric inhaled deeply and exhaled, trying to contain his annoyance. He jerked his head in Emmett's direction and answered the question in Tristan's eyes. "He just made me a promise, okay? He promised to help me out with something, one way or another. Nothing you need to concern yourself with. Now take my hand and accept my fucking apology, will you? I don't do it often. I shit on you and I shouldn't have. I had no right. I'm sorry." His voice was gravel rough and his face was still red, his head pounding but his tone was sincere. He had fucked up and didn't mind admitting it. He stood there, patiently waiting with his hand outstretched.

Finally, Tristan stepped forward. His eyes were steady on Terric's face and he palmed the demon's hand. His disappointment was evident. For a second he had seen a way out of the shit he lived in, day after day. For it to be so close and then snatched away was merely more torture. He glared over at Emmett, then Terric and back at the cop. He spoke quietly, his voice serious. "You did me no favor there, demon. None at all. I welcome an end, and I am guessing Terric does as well. You had no right to interfere."

Emmett studied the hybrid closely, his eyes sharp as he picked through every facet of the vampire's mind. Tristan, for his part, didn't try to block any of it. He stood there, arms at his side and shame laid bare for the demon to see firsthand. Emmett withdrew and regarded the man before him for several moments. Finally, he said, not unkindly, "So, fuck the consequences, for both of you then, right? Do you know the price you would have to pay, and that he will be paying twice as much, both of you stuck there for fucking eternity? Existing here sucks and hurts and we all long for it to end at one time or another, but the alternative is so much worse. Jesus, Terric's spent quality time there. He can tell you. We all have, so why he would sign up for it willingly, I don't understand. Anyways, you want to die, vampire? Find someone else to handle that for you. Or better yet, take care of it yourself. You know, it could be so much worse. Of course, you'll see that for yourself, sooner rather than later, unfortunately. I'll see you later, kid."

When Tristan opened his eyes once more, Emmett was gone. Terric was staring at him solemnly, his eyes sad, as he saw what Emmett had just foreshadowed; he had gone into the other demon's mind and simply took what he wanted to see. Emmett was able to see the future, not every detail but the inevitable outcome. What he had seen in Tristan's had caused him to pause, and the silence had been enough to draw Terric's notice. Considering the way the demon had just spent several minutes denying Terric oxygen, Terric hadn't felt too bad about trespassing, loudly and painfully into the man's head. Terric's gaze on Tristan was filled with sorrow, and he swallowed hard before speaking. "The offer of a ride still open? Can you drop me at the lighthouse?" Tristan nodded, and they left the club.

Not much was said on the ride. The silence wasn't awkward, though. Both were merely lost in the events of the night. When the truck pulled to a stop, both men stepped out. Tristan handed Terric the keys, insisting on shifting and running home. Terric understood that need, one he himself had to surrender to fairly often. He watched the wolf streak out of the parking lot, heading into the woods. Terric's head whipped around as awareness hit him. He wasn't alone. Another wolf was nearby. Smaller than he when he was in wolf form, but not by much. He eyed it warily and kept a respectful distance. The wolf's lip pulled back, revealing huge canines, lethally sharp. Terric stood motionless, his eyes not meeting the wolf's gaze head on. Finally, the wolf bolted to the woods, but not far. He heard rustling around, felt the charge in the air as the wolf shifted form. Out from the woods stepped a male, pulling jeans over his hips, his stare leveled on Terric. It was him. Kevin.

Chapter Eight

TERRIC STOOD FROZEN, the alcohol intensifying the buzzing sound in his head, giving a surreal quality to the moment. He fumbled for something to say, a way to lend normalcy to what should be a casual encounter. Jordyn's words replayed in his mind, her urging him to be himself. Jesus, his heart was racing and he was ashamed of the fear pounding through him. He pictured her, as she was last time he saw her. Triumphant and proud. She was braver than he was. The thought had him squaring his shoulders and for the second time that evening, he stuck out his hand.

"Kevin, right? Terric. Just came here to..." His voice trailed off. What had he come to the lighthouse for? To dwell on shit. To castigate himself for letting her go and not giving her what she needed. For not being able to be her mate in the truest sense of the word. He thought for a moment, and realized that letting Jordyn go had been him giving her what she needed.

Still. He wasn't ready for this. He needed to talk to the man, prove to himself that he could do it. It wouldn't go any further though. Even if Kevin were interested, Terric was a fucking train wreck. He had nothing to offer anyone. He realized that Kevin had taken his hand, and now Terric had held on to it longer than was customary, lost in thought. He dropped Kevin's hand, took a half step back. "I don't know why I'm here, to be honest. Needed to think, I guess."

Kevin nodded, his hand warm from where his palm had come into contact with Terric's. He stared for a moment, wondering what caused a man to be so… lost. The only word he could think of to describe the man before him, was lost, maybe bereft. Many other descriptors came to mind, but all were eclipsed by the look in the man's eyes, the bewildered, sad gaze. He cast about for something to say, anything to keep the man from leaving right away. "Yeah, it's important. Time to be alone, to think. I know. I just needed a place to run, something less familiar than the woods by my clinic. I like the beach; the lighthouse always makes me feel better. Centers me, I guess. Not to be presumptuous, but it looks like you could use that. Being centered, I mean. You seem a bit… ah…" He stopped, unwilling to insinuate himself where he shouldn't tread. Everything about the man screamed 'back off!' He wanted to accommodate that, but not back too far off. This man interested him.

"Adrift." Kevin was surprised when Terric filled in the blank for him. He lifted his eyes to meet the demon's gaze as he listened intently to what Terric said. He had a feeling the taciturn man didn't open up often. He remained silent as Terric continued.

"Honestly, I think that's the only word that fits. I feel like I've been set fucking adrift and I don't know why I'm telling you this. I don't know what to grab onto and I am fucking drunk still. Man, I'm sorry, and I appreciate you trying to talk to me, but I don't do this. I don't talk, to anyone. But especially not other men. I'm picking up on your vibe, Kevin, and I know you're interested. I don't do men, okay?"

Terric made himself meet Kevin's stare at that last part. Trying to infuse truth into the statement. When Kevin laughed, he scowled, his anger growing in proportion to the frustration he was feeling at being called out. He ground out, "Don't know what the fuck is so amusing. I have a female, and she's..." Jesus, was he to the point he would actually fucking lie? He despised lies. Lying was a poor-spirited and chicken shit move. "I did have a female. She's gone. Left. Still. This is ridiculous and I don't have time for this. Not interested. There. Simple answer."

Kevin actually felt sorry for Terric. The laughter had been a reflex, and part of his smartass automatic response. He stepped up closer, a half smile on his face. He spoke softly, his voice gentle. "Terric-I'm not going to deny that I'm interested. Clearly you can read people, so lying would be pointless, even if I were inclined to do so. I'm not, though. I'm comfortable with who and what I am, and I don't need anyone's approval for anything I do. You apparently do. I don't know who you are trying to impress or who you're trying to hide from. Frankly, I don't care. I don't bother involving myself in other people's business. I also make it a rule not to fuck around with people still hiding. It's far more of a pain in the ass than it's worth, for me, anyways. I'm not interested in being someone's experimental stage. I'm sorry your girl left. I can see you're upset and that you love her. Tell you what? For whatever reason, I find myself still interested, even though you have far too much baggage for my liking.

I'm one of the only vets here in Ptown. Give it some time and then come find me." Kevin didn't give Terric a chance to respond before he turned and walked away, heading to the little sports car that Terric hadn't even noticed when they had pulled into the parking lot. That wasn't a surprise, though. His eyes had been closed and he had been fighting a wave of dizziness from the alcohol/loss of air combo back at the club.

Terric watched him back out of the spot and shoot out of the lot, hearing the smooth roar of the engine. It had been a sleek little Jag, and Terric had winced at the sight of it. Useless car. What would a vet want with a car like that, worthless for hauling around animals, and a nightmare on farm roads. He shrugged, trying to push the encounter out of his mind. It didn't happen. He was still replaying it in his head as he walked down to the water's edge. His boots were sinking in the sand, making walking a pain in the ass. He pulled them off, followed by his socks, and dropped them down into the sand, settling on his ass beside them. The sun was starting to rise, and he marveled at how much had happened since he had been here last. How was it possible that in less than forty-eight hours, he had lost everything, and had his life turned completely upside down?

A FAMILIAR FEELING landed deep in the pit of his stomach. A ball of dread that only signaled one thing. He was to be summoned soon. He felt his fire brand heat up, and his hand covered it, rubbing lightly. Likely the incident with the vampire and then Emmett had brought it on. Exhaustion had his body slumped in on itself, making him appear older. He was essentially ageless, would always look anywhere between thirty to forty years old, but although he couldn't grow old, he could show stress, fatigue, any strong emotion, really. He lay back in the sand, arms akimbo and eyes closed. His breathing grew deeper, slowing to the point that one could perhaps chance upon him and think him dead, not breathing at all.

Terric's mind began to wander, contemplating recent events. His body was not his own at the moment as it slipped into a state not unlike hibernation. His limbs were heavy, too heavy for him to move. He let his mind drift. It helped him not fight uselessly against what he couldn't change.

There is sorrow in the demons, whoever thought otherwise was grievously wrong, either by choice or out of blindness. Being a demon didn't render one incapable of emotion. Indeed, they often felt not only their own emotion, but that of those they cared about, those with whom they shared a bond, as well as those whose souls they were taking, their intended victims. His love and caring of Jordyn, even without the mated bond, meant that she held court in a corner of his heart. Terric felt her there; her past that had damaged her, had also changed a piece of him. He knew and understood happiness, having experienced it a few times in his life. Not happiness, perhaps. Contentment, brief moments of peace.

He could see and extrapolate, from those times, what true joy would feel like. He had seen it in the hearts of others. In fact, it had saved many of his intended targets from a swift death and painful afterlife. Terric pondered that, what the souls trapped in the other realm endured. He wondered if it were worth it, just to have an end to the torment of a so-called life.

When he opened his eyes, he was there, in the other realm. No one above ground would have seen him disappear. It would have been as if he had turned to vapor and misted out of sight, imperceptible to the human eye. They may have seen the sort of ripple that comes from the pavement during a steamy summer afternoon. Nothing more.

Terric sighed heavily, mentally preparing. When summoned, not much leeway would be granted in regard to time allotted to show himself. Upon arrival, he would not be able to shift, at first because of the presence of silver and iron in each chamber and throughout the realm. And then, as he grew more exhausted, he would be unable to retain any form at all and would be reduced to his mere essence. His wolf would fight this, at first. He could feel the wolf snarling, raging mindlessly against the intrusions and tortures soon to be inflicted upon his demon side. The wolf would feel the demon's suffering and try to save it, and in doing so, would ensure demon suffered more to pay for the wolf's sins.

It would feel as if the fiber of his being were being torn asunder, until finally, the wolf would howl endlessly and then submit. That was the hardest part, feeling that part of himself lay down and admit defeat. He would weep for this part of himself, this proud wolf. The tears would fall as he offered a silent apology to the wolf, apologizing for this part of who he was. The demon would show no outward sign of this, determined not to draw out any suffering the wolf would be subjected to.

As time dragged on there, the demon would lose the ability to see, to hear, to reason. The only thing he would not lose would be the ability to feel. If a demon died during this, he was simply brought back to life, endlessly, until the master felt that the scales were once again tipped in his favor, for the demon could never be ahead of the master.

Terric didn't need to appear before the demon master to accept his punishment, technically. Such could be delivered anywhere, in any realm. The punishment mainly took place inside him; his mind, his heart. Particularly his heart. He could feel it, a sort of fragility that had not been a part of who he was before. He was in some sort of flux, between his time with Jordyn and what would come next. His mind flashed briefly to Kevin and he quickly shoved the thought away. Not the time to think upon that, to have Kevin's visage in his head when the master took his thoughts.

Although he didn't physically have to have a demon in the other realm for the punishment, the master still preferred to summon his demons. Not to collect them, but to summon them. So Terric had to deliver himself unto the one who owned him, for his master liked to be hands on, so to speak. He wanted to be there to see the punishment endured; to feel and feed off the agony of emotions a demon went through. All demons ended up submitting to his master's demand for supplication at some time or another. Such was the nature of their existence.

Some say that it is just to give them a taste of the ultimate punishment that awaited all demons as they stood before God and his angels for final judgment. Terric wondered at that, often. He had never met the one the humans referred to as their Heavenly Father, but he would like to. Even if it meant eternity in suffering, he wanted the chance to stand before this Father and receive this judgment. He truly wanted to know if he was to blame for his nature, for what he was. If one was cursed from birth, how could one be judged because of that? He had tried from the time he was able to reason to live his life ethically, to hunt judiciously, to use what he did to rid the world of monsters worse than himself. If his nature was such that there would be no redemption for him, then he wanted to stand before this Father and receive this sentence sooner, rather than later. Right away, in fact.

When Terric arrived in the other realm, his demeanor was calm and his pace unhurried. He strode down the familiar corridor, nodding respectfully at some as he passed. Others earned his direct scorn. Some beings were so evil even another demon couldn't fathom or abide them. The air was dank, damp, and cooler than one would expect. Actually, not much different than the feeling one experienced when walking down into a cave, the smells changing as the descent steepened. He felt himself angle back slightly to compensate for the sloping floor, his boots scraping against the rough stone.

The lighting was poor, not that it affected his sight. It made for interesting patterns in the shadows thrown on the walls. They danced and writhed, and one could nearly see the souls that suffered there. Mouths opened in agonized screams, more frustrating because of the fruitlessness of the gesture. Locked forever in the silent scream experienced during a nightmare. Similarly, the tortured soul felt the crushing terror of running, feet pounding the ground and heart hammering in exertion, only to find that they had not moved an inch and the threat was no farther away.

Terric saw all of this and none of it. It had lost the ability to affect him overmuch. Just as anyone confronted with daily tragedy, he had become desensitized. The souls that spent eternity trapped here had made the choices that led to this. Likely, many had not had a chance to redeem themselves, but that was the way of it. Some decisions could not be undone, no way to tip the balance back in favor of their victims, the evil that had been brought down here to dwell for the remainder of forever had no redeeming qualities.

Balance couldn't always be achieved, but justice would be sought. And there would be no chance that this kind of evil could perpetrate itself in the light of day again. Unfortunately, new evil was born every day, thus assuring that demons like Terric and the one who held mastery over them would always exist as well. He sighed, thinking on that last item. Always existing.

Fuck, but he was tired. He wasn't ready to die just then, but the possibility that he would one day die was not unappealing. He could die, but only with permission. Technically, he had died many times already, but only so that he could suffer and be brought back. And know firsthand that even his death was not his, even that belonged to someone else. Slavery was as old as the dawn of time, and he was no different than any of the other demons. Owned. He may not have believed he had a soul, but what made him who he was, his essence, as it were, could be rebirthed and reformed into any physical body. If the damage to his current physical body weren't too great, his healing powers were as remarkable any other paranormal creature.

His wolf grumbled loudly, clearly unhappy with the line his thoughts had taken. Terric had continued his descent. The cavernous room he had passed through had brought with it a change in temperature. Still, it didn't feel as hot as one would as expect, if fables were to be believed. Then again, the flames weren't for him. The flames that consumed the damned naturally raised the ambient temperature, but they only burned those who they were intended for. He thought briefly on Lucas. His scars would never fade completely, but the bastard had been lucky to retain his human form at all.

There was a sharp whine, soul deep inside him. Terric paused, and the wolf inside him did as well. Instead of hunkering down to wait out their time down here, the wolf was restless, edgy and ready to fight. Terric drew deep breaths and forced his heart rate lower, his eyes closing as he focused his thoughts inward. Searching... searching for the cause or the source of the disquiet within himself. The wolf, that side of his nature was fighting a losing battle. The wolf's pacing became faster, until he felt like his own skin would explode. Something was off, different. His physiological responses were becoming that of the wolf's instead of the man, and he was losing control over them.

He struggled not to panic and not to give in to the call to shift. No, fuck *no!* The wolf would never survive down here. It had never been an issue, before. He wouldn't have been able to shift even if he had wanted to. He swallowed hard and looked around, knowing there was no point to doing so. Whether he appeared alone or not, eyes were on him, on everyone, always. He began to backtrack, hoping desperately to make it above ground before he shifted. His hands began to shake and he was sweating. He had never had to fight this before, it had always been a natural part of who he was and he gladly gave himself over to the freedom it brought him. Not now though, not now, when it would spell anything but freedom.

Free will was gone. One minute he was struggling for control and the next he was shifting, giving himself over to it before he realized. He stood, shook out his fur and tried to categorize what was still his to command of his body and what was now theirs. A sharp whine rose from him, pain lancing through his entire being. He moved forward as he was bade to do, his tail hanging low enough to brush the rough stone ground as he trotted down the slope, compelled by unseen forces.

When he arrived at the location, he knew immediately why he was there. Several other wolves were there, and they had come to the same realization. Terric revolted, his limbs locking and his nails digging into the ground to try to gain purchase. It didn't matter. He could try to put the brakes on as much as he wanted; it was a temporary and foolish reprieve. He lay down on the ground, his eyes closed and he tried to give himself over to the one who decided such things. He cautiously opened his eyes, hoping his petition had been granted and that he was in another chamber. The pain would be intense but it wouldn't destroy him as the scene in the cavern likely would.

He had been denied. Terric rolled to his belly; his ears pinned to his head and angled downward, as he surveyed the other wolves. This was the one thing they all avoided, at all costs. Demons were not known for their heart or their kindness for any save a select few beings close to them. But the hybrids, the shifters, they all respected the animal that dwelt inside the other beings.

That was irrelevant here. They would do what they were commanded to do. They were made for this reason. It would serve several purposes. They would be doing what was essentially their job, what they were charged to do. Along with that though, it would be torture for the wolves involved, and would serve as a lesson. They were not free, and they were not supposed to feel. The fact that they were shifters, the animal part of their nature made them weaker; they were vulnerable because they felt. They had compassion, formed bonds, and fell in love. This was to remind them that doing so was a dangerous mistake.

Terric moved closer to the others, his eyes stopping and resting on each wolf in turn. Yes, these were friends, for the most part. Many were ones he had run with, trusting the other being enough to shift in front of them, becoming more vulnerable if one had decided to play false and shift back. In wolf form, there would have been less of a defense against one in a demon form. Among them were faces he had seen and cared about.

The atmosphere changed. His fur stood on end and he rose, his head hanging low, close to the ground and his lip curling up in a vicious snarl. He felt his eyes change and his ears straightened, tipped forward. At some unseen signal, all the wolves moved ahead, to a central target. The scene was primal, and intense, once they gave up trying to escape the command.

They fought each other to reach the one, each wolf eager to claim victory over the one to be eliminated. Terric was no less feral than the rest. His teeth sank into flesh, tearing muscle and hitting bone and he shook his head. It felt good, giving himself over to the animal. He felt the teeth as they sank into his leg, missing vital tendons but causing him to yelp sharply and jerk on it, trying to remove it from the other wolf's mouth.

It went on for hours it seemed. He would see a wolf drop, either in exhaustion or due to injuries too severe to continue fighting. None would die save the one that was supposed to, but all would wish they were that one. The fight was down to him and another against the target, whose strength was flagging. The eyes of the falling wolf met those of the ones charged with restoring balance. He dropped, his legs crumbling beneath him and still Terric and the other wolf hybrid continued, single-minded in their determination.

Killing him was actually a kindness, a relatively quick death at the hands of other wolves, friends. He would have the rest of eternity to answer for his crimes. In that moment, his eyes met first Terric's and then the other wolf, understanding and empathy there in the dying wolf's expression. He knew they suffered, would continue to suffer long after his physical body gave up. He stopped fighting and Terric's jaw relaxed slightly; loosening the grip he had on its throat to see if air was dragged in to flood the lungs with oxygen. Nothing. Terric shook his head and the wolf was like a rag doll. Terric opened his mouth completely and released the wolf, backing away and dropping down to his haunches. The other wolf approached cautiously, crouching in a submissive bow. Terric nudged him once, and then threw his head back and howled for the length of several heart beats until exhaustion forced him to stop. He dropped his head down on his paws, blood drying around his muzzle. And there he waited, unmoving as he felt the other wolf drop beside him to do the same.

Only one wolf would die that day, but all the others would wish it were them to have received such a gift. Terric closed his eyes and let sleep take him. For this brief reprieve, he gave no thought to Kevin, Jordyn, nothing. He didn't ruminate on what his existence meant; exhaustion granted him mercy in that it let his mind truly rest for a while.

Chapter Nine

WHEN TERRIC AWOKE, he was in wolf form, but no
longer in the other realm. He had no memory of
leaving, and as he lifted his head and looked around, Terric
could tell that the others were in much the same state. That
was the odd part. They were all still in their wolf form, which
meant that their wolves had been manipulated. The thought
pissed him off, brutally so. He stood and shook out his fur,
his eyes on each wolf in turn. No one challenged him; no one
wanted vengeance for a fallen friend in the other realm. If
anything, they were all going out of their way to leave a
respectful distance between each other. After several measured breaths, each turned and began to walk away. Tails were
low to the ground, and each left alone, save one mated pair.

Terric stayed wolf, and after a while, he started to run. The
bunching and stretching of his muscles was a welcome
change. His stride lengthened. For the briefest moment all
paws were off the ground as he tried to put as much distance
between where he had been and where he was heading. He
had no clear destination at first, just wanted miles covered.

The wolf lifted his head, sniffing the air as he slowed. The ocean, he recognized the scent and his heart raced, knowing where he needed to be. He moved with purpose, sharp eyes scanning for any sort of threat as he headed to the lighthouse. No one around was around; he was able to move close without a problem. He was sitting there, next to the structure for cover as much as to remain grounded in the present.

He felt a shift in the air, a familiar scent approaching. His head swung around, and his eyes rested on Adam, the lighthouse keeper. Man and beast stared at each other for several minutes. They knew each other, vaguely, these two. Adam's story was familiar to Terric, even though Adam didn't understand it himself. Adam's eyes were steady as he took in the wolf, and then the immortal human nodded. He spoke quietly, calmly, and told Terric he'd leave him alone, just wanted to let him know another wolf that had been watching Terric while he had stared out to sea, lost in thought.

Terric blinked, unaware how much time had passed and cognizant of the fact that he was allowing himself to be in danger with his inattention. He let his senses spread out, sharpening his focus and then he turned, his lip peeling back off his sharp canine as the other wolf approached. Although slightly smaller than Terric, the wolf was pure shifter. It meant that in wolf form, he would be more powerful than Terric, a hybrid. Terric stood, his hackles rising and his ears close to his head as he let out a warning growl.

The wolf looked at him, unfazed. He dropped into a puppy-like bow, playfully showing submission. When that gained no favorable reaction, he rolled over on his back; his belly exposed and gave Terric a comedic canine grin. Terric let out a sigh, resisting the urge to shake his head. He inhaled deeply, memorizing the scent. Kevin's scent… Terric must have given off some signal that he wasn't out to rip the other wolf's head off, because Kevin righted himself, leapt up and bumped his nose lightly onto Terric's shoulder, nudging and then running a few paces, trying to challenge Terric into giving chase. Finally, he turned around and nipped the thick scruff of fur around Terric's throat. Not enough to damage or start a true fight, just enough that it couldn't be ignored. Kevin turned and bounded off, gaining a considerable lead. Terric dug his claws into the sand, a high-pitched bark leaving him involuntarily as he forgot about the shit that brought him to this place and simply enjoyed the moment.

They covered miles within minutes, turning and running back along the surf. The sun was dipping low on the horizon by the time they finally stopped. Some silent communication passed between them and then they both shifted back. Kevin turned to his car and grabbed a pair of sweat pants, tossing a pair to Terric before tugging his own on. Terric shrugged and drew them up over his hips. They were nearly the same size.

Kevin nodded to Terric and simply said, "Call me" before jumping in his car and driving away. There was no time for Terric to reply, not that he had a reply ready. He watched the car until as it drove out of sight, trying to imagine what he would say, if he did call the shifter. Nothing in him knew how to love and be loved in the normal sense, even just relating to others was a challenge at times.

What he had with Jordyn had been more about caring for and protecting someone weaker than himself. He loved so many things about her, but it was more of a love based on functionality. They had each served a purpose in each other's lives and they worked. He didn't know how to be in someone's life if he didn't need to be there. What was the purpose of calling Kevin? To go on a date?

Terric didn't date. That was a foreign concept. It seemed frivolous and awkward and exactly the type of situation that would highlight every flaw and fault he had and set it on display. Kevin was clearly well educated, a doctor like his brother. Terric had no need of furthering his education, so a clear disparity would exist in the way they could communicate. Kevin knew who and what he was and was clearly fine with that. Terric didn't know if he could ever truly be who he was.

He thought about that for a moment. He tried to imagine sex with another man. He never really let himself consider it; he would never have considered cheating on Jordyn. Their relationship may not have been based on true love or on forever or even on the truth, but he would never have lied to her. Together, they lied to the outside world, but to each other they shared brutal honesty.

Disrespecting her by lying with another would have been out of the question. And she had been the same toward him, she knew his temper and that he didn't share, not that she had ever been tempted. He sighed, and returned to his previous thoughts, knowing he was avoiding the issue even in his mind. When he tried to imagine sex with another man, he couldn't imagine anything beyond what he had already experienced. Sex was a weapon in the other realm, one commonly used to punish, and to reinforce the fact of a demon's subservience to higher ranking demons. He pictured the encounters, cursing his memory and perfect recollection of the details. Chances were slim that he would be able to be physically intimate with another man, ever.

SEVERAL DAYS PASSED, before he decided to go home. When he arrived back at his apartment, he parked and headed up the stairs, refusing to look at the empty parking spot where Jordyn's car would have been. It frustrated him, that he was apparently not as well adjusted as she was. The last they had spoken, she had claimed to be doing well. He had offered to feed her, and she had agreed to call him when she was in need. She had been upbeat, mentioning a couple of females she had become friendly with. Apparently one was human and the other was vampire. The three of them enjoyed hanging out and doing girl stuff together, and it had truly made Terric smile to hear the excitement in Jordy's voice. Until she had softly asked him what he had been up to.

Terric had tried to answer her in a vague way, and then finally gave up and made an excuse to end the call. She had been texting him since he had returned from the other realm, and he knew he couldn't stall forever. He had to call her back. She had a sense of when he was called to the other realm, and apparently distance hadn't dulled it.

As he was walking up the stairs, he pulled his phone from his pocket and called, feeling like a coward for hoping it went to voicemail. And since he had never been particularly lucky, it didn't and she answered on the second ring. She didn't even say hello. "Are you okay?" The sentence came out more as a demand than a question. She had always worried about him.

Terric finished unlocking his door and dropped his keys in the bowl as he headed into the apartment. He told her he was as he grabbed a beer and made his way over to the couch. She hadn't said anything while he moved about, and he knew from experience that she would sit there in silence forever, waiting for him to continue. Stubborn. And like that, he found himself grinning for a moment, missing this side of her and glad to see she hadn't changed.

He gave a mock sigh and tried to figure out how to answer her. "I really am fine, Jordy. This time was different, no... punishment. Not for me, not physically, anyway. A wolf needed elimination. Well, a wolf like me. So they had us all there in wolf form." At her sharp inhale, he closed his eyes and was at once both grateful and homesick for her. She understood without being told. She knew what that would have done to him emotionally. He continued on after a moment. "Jordyn, I really am okay. It sucked, and I hated it, it would have been easier if it were me on the receiving end, to be honest. And I have no choice but to be honest with you, even now. It just pisses me off, but I survived, and now I just want to forget it. When I came back, I stayed wolf, and it was good. There was another shifter, and we ran together. It helped."

Jordyn sat on the other end, her eyes sad as she pictured the beautiful wolf being forced to do things that would kill his spirit, in a realm he never should have been in. If she could change anything in the world, it would be that. And she knew that by making Terric not a demon, she would be changing who he was. She had gone over all the arguments and ramifications in her head over the years, even knowing the fruitlessness of it. She couldn't change what he was any more than she could change who she was.

Still, the idea of saving him from anything that could hurt him had been appealing. One of the little fantasies she used to indulge in, rather than focus on fixing herself. She would pretend that she had the power to save those she loved. Her child, her parents, her brother, and then Terric. In real life,

Jordyn hadn't been able to save anyone, even herself, but in her fantasies, she was strong and powerful and could change the world. Something caught her attention, some slight change in his tone, a quietness at the end that told her that something important wasn't being said. She thought about how far to push, and knew not far.

Terric on a regular day was closed off, but when he was hurting he became impossible to approach. She kept her tone light when she asked if the shifter had been down in the other realm with him. Terric told her no, that he was pure shifter. He. Jordyn's heart leapt at the thought that maybe T would finally move on and find out who he was supposed to be. A thousand questions ran through her mind, and she wanted nothing more than to run back to Provincetown to make Terric tell her every detail. It would have been pointless, however. That just wasn't who he was. She sighed, knowing too, that he craved solitude when he first came back. That made it even more important, the fact that he had stayed wolf and hung out with this other shifter.

Jordyn lay back on her couch, and pictured him on the couch in their old apartment. Terric's apartment now. She could imagine him perfectly. He would have been sitting forward at first, legs open with his arms resting on his knees. He always paid attention when she spoke to him. She never felt like a bother, telling him how she felt about even the stupidest of things. He would look at her, his eye contact comforting and constant, making her feel important in his world. He never laughed at her, mocked her, or spoke down to her. He acted like what she had to say wasn't stupid or pointless. His patience was endless and he had given her a softness that he didn't think he possessed.

To the rest of the world, he could be cold. Some would say mean, heartless, ruthless. He was all of those things, at times, she supposed. Never with her, though. And he was never like that with anyone weaker than he was. Even when he was eliminating someone, taking their soul, he derived no pleasure and he was humane where possible. He wouldn't have said so and would likely argue with her for saying it. It seemed as if he didn't want anyone to know what was inside him. Which was a shame. What was inside the demon was beautiful.

They spoke for a few more minutes, and she could hear the restlessness in his voice. Only for her, would he sit and chat on the phone. She smiled sadly, missing him so much it became a physical ache. She loved where she was and she loved that she was trying, and making progress. But she wasn't strong enough just yet. And the allure of running home, having him wrap those strong arms around her was too great. She swallowed, strove to keep her tone light when she said she needed to be going. He told her he would talk to her soon and then he spoke to her in that voice that reached deep inside her and gently wrapped around her heart. He had disconnected the call before she allowed herself to answer, whispering softly, "I love you, too, T."

Chapter Ten

LIFE BEGAN TO resume, and he shook off the effects of the other realm fairly quickly. Terric poured himself into his work, making some changes but doing so slowly so as not to have a mutiny on his hands. People, whether they were immortal or human, resisted change. He wasn't overly concerned with his own popularity, but he did want to keep his headaches down to a minimum. He trained the new staff he hired personally, as he didn't believe in letting people learn bad habits that he would have to break later. And the solitude, after so long being part of a couple, wasn't terrible. Before Jordyn, he had actually preferred it. He told himself he just needed to grow accustomed to it once more.

He had things he wanted to try, and being part of a couple hadn't been conducive to that. At least, that's what he told himself. He wasn't an educated man, but for some reason, he wanted to try to write, something he hadn't shared with her, and in a way, he wished he had. It felt like he had held a part of himself from her, a sort of dishonesty or selfishness of spirit. He had no excuse not to do it now, or at least try. He likely had no business doing it. He didn't know much about things like sentence structure and grammar. But he had stories in his head. Many of them were borne of time spent in the other realm, a way to keep his mind busy and the wolf entertained, distracted.

When he walked into the apartment, he realized he once again would need to shop. Fine for him to browbeat Jordyn into finding out who she was. He needed to do the same himself. The light from the fridge cut through the dark kitchen. He grabbed a beer, cracking it and draining nearly half before he paused to search for food. It didn't take long to realize that unless he wanted cocktail sauce on crackers again, he needed to go out to eat and stop at a grocery store on his way home. He had only been living alone a couple months but the place was already appearing desolate, as if a woman's touch had never graced it. He wasn't lonely, didn't feel depressed, but his place seemed to tell a different story. Terric glanced around once more and then headed into the bedroom to change his clothes. He pulled on clean jeans, a deep blue button down flannel shirt, and grabbed his only decent boots. He picked up his keys and headed out the door, inhaling deeply as he stepped into the crisp air.

The truck was loud in a comforting, steady way. He was used to the way it rumbled when he gave it gas, the slight shake if he asked for too much speed too quickly. The interior smelled familiar, and he knew precisely when he needed to stop for gas and if the engine was running too hot. There was nothing he couldn't predict about driving it, except other drivers. Terric was pulling in to the parking lot of Mulligan's when someone cut him off from the opposite direction, clipping his bumper.

He stopped short, brakes protesting the harsh treatment while his tires squealed against the pavement, even at the slow speed he had been going. The truck was heavy as fuck, one of the things he liked about it. The compact foreign piece of shit didn't stop, and that's when he grew pissed. He watched it turn around the back of the restaurant. And he stomped on the gas to follow, irritation turning to fury as a finger came out of the driver's side window and flipped him off. The other driver must have been too busy being a cocky asshole and forgot he was supposed to be steering, because he plowed into a parked car. Another foreign number, but this one considerably more flashy and expensive. Kevin's car.

Terric wondered briefly if he had come back to this place on purpose, this place he met Kevin the first time. He didn't have time to think about it, all that went on in some obscure part of his brain while the rest was busy deciding how he was going to hurt the asshole driving.

T leapt out of his truck, his arm reaching into the still open window of the small car. A drunken human man sat inside, a chronic alcoholic judging by the red bulbous nose and noxious scent of alcohol seeping out of his pores. His hand closed into a fist around the cheap material of the man's shirt, his eyes cold, the color slowly deepening as they did before they turned red. He had no desire to steal this one's soul; it was simply plain rage that had him fired up. He was about to drag the man out of the window of his car, when he felt a restraining hand on his arm. Terric's head whipped around, but he didn't release the human. Kevin stared at him, eyes level and then he broke out into a cocky grin, chuckling lightly.

Terric frowned; about to growl at the shifter to get lost,

and then Kevin spoke. "You care about my car that much? I'm touched. He's not worth it. Let it go. Besides, we've company." Kevin nodded his head in the direction of the diner, and Terric sighed, cursing softly under his breath.

Emmett strolled over, and the demon was on duty, in full cop mode. The human, who had been silent during most of the exchange, also cursed. Terric almost felt bad for him. He could read the human's thoughts, and it was almost comical. The guy was trying to decide what was worse, another DWI or an ass beating. T let go of the human and stepped back, nodding at Emmett. He watched as Kevin gave Emmett his information, and it occurred to him that the shifter was calm. His demeanor spoke of someone in control of his emotions and possessing full knowledge of who and what he was; he was exceedingly comfortable with himself. And Terric realized just how appealing that was. He tilted his head, studying the shifter carefully.

Kevin turned and approached and they stood together, watching Emmett load the human into the back of his patrol car and take off. Kevin peered over at Terric, and when he spoke, it was with quiet authority in his tone. "I'd say let's go inside and have something to eat, nice and public. Keep you from getting spooked and taking off again, or being all defensive on me again. I'm not going to though. You aren't the type for games and neither am I. You look like shit. We'll go back to my place. I'm a decent cook. I'll make you dinner, and we can talk for a while. Alone. Private. You can drive me in your ancient ass truck, since my car looks like shit. I'll have them tow it to a shop tomorrow." His eyes met Terric's, and he gave a challenging smirk. "Come on. What's the worst that can happen?"

Terric drew in a deep breath and stared off into the night. He released the breath slowly, nodding. "Yeah. Okay, yeah, that works." He turned back to the truck and got in, waiting for Kevin to get in the other side. They drove around the parking lot in silence, and then Kevin told him to make a right, and another at the second light. Terric drove, and then peered out of the corner of his eye at his passenger. Kevin's profile was strong, and his presence in the truck was comfortable, not intrusive as Terric had thought it would be. He caught Kevin checking out the interior of the truck, a funny look on his face. "What?"

KEVIN FLASHED A grin. "This thing is really fucking old."

TERRIC LAUGHED, RELAXING further. "Yeah, well. It has character. You can barely tell where that asshole hit it, and yours has to be carried out of that parking lot."

KEVIN SHOT BACK, not missing a beat. "You can hardly tell because this thing was already a heap. I'll take class over character when it comes to what I drive."

THEY ARGUED GOOD-NATUREDLY back and forth. The tension eased. Each boasted the merits of their particular vehicle, with Kevin giving directions as they went. Finally, they pulled into a long, winding driveway. The property sat on the edge of Provincetown, probably not even part of the town proper, more like an unincorporated section. Kevin had a lot of land, enough for his practice and a few fenced-in acres. Terric looked over the place, noting the dense woods that edged it, and knew it would be a good spot to run without worry. He set the emergency brake in front of the large house and then sat for a moment behind the wheel, quiet once more.

Kevin lightly touched his arm. "Let's go." Terric watched him as he stepped down, shutting the door behind him and walking toward the house. Not glancing back, confident Terric would follow. It irritated him at the same time as it made it easier for him to open his own door, hearing it squeak loudly as a reminder to oil the hinge. He slammed the door, shoved his keys in his pocket, and walked up the steps into the home.

Kevin called to him, presumably from the kitchen. Terric followed, walking deeper into the house and taking in details as he went. The home was huge, too big for one person. He came to the kitchen, noting the cheerful yet masculine decor. Kevin was already digging ingredients out of the fridge, laying items on the counter as he went. He opened a beer and offered it to Terric, then grabbed one for himself.

T settled with his back leaning against the granite island, watching Kevin as he set about making the meal. He was browning some ground meat, and headed over to the cabinet, grabbed a package of buns. The smells had Terric's stomach grumbling, and he was suddenly starving. Kevin dropped some seasoning into the meat, stirred a couple times and then turned around and grabbed a couple plates. He set two buns on each plate, heaped a ton of beef onto each, and then placed the top bun on them, handing Terric a plate with a triumphant grin. "Dinner."

Terric laughed. "Sloppy Joes. Not bad. Character over class, I like it. Not what I would have guessed you being into. This place is pretty classy looking, your house. Kind of big for one person." He accepted the plate and followed Kevin over to the table, setting his beer down before returning to the fridge and grabbing them each another. He realized as he turned back to the table it was a pretty damn familiar move, his first time at the man's house, but Kevin smiled his thanks and didn't comment on it, so he let it go, reminding himself to relax.

Kevin finished his first beer and set the empty aside. "My brothers have both lived here at one time or another. Sometimes all of us at once. You know Dane. Seth is different. He's quite a bit older, and difficult. He stays in Ireland for the most part. He has some... likability issues, you might say. He still will crash here once in a while, but he has some issues with my "lifestyle". He's a drunk, often a mean one. Truly, he's not a bad guy. He's just kind of lost. Hell, they both are. I was too, until I came out. I don't advertise my sexuality, but I don't go out of my way to hide it, either. Dane is more accepting, but then, we grew up together. He's only a couple years older than me. They are both hybrids, vampire shifters. I'm the only one who is just a shifter. No clue why, but I think it's why Seth hates me at times. I know it's why my father did. I took after my mother. I am nothing of him, as he reminded me constantly growing up. Anyway, you may run into Seth around town sometime. You'll understand what I mean then."

Terric tried to imagine what that would be like, an outcast in one's own family. He told Kevin a little bit about his own upbringing, just the basics. His mother was also a shifter, his father a demon. It had been so long since he had spoken of them, he didn't really know what to say, so he kept it short. Kevin didn't push, understanding Terric wasn't the type to talk about many things. The talk turned to lighter subjects.

Terric asked Kevin about his work.

They ate as they talked, and Terric watched the expression on Kevin's face when he talked about his job. He clearly loved the animals. A large wolf hybrid was laying on the couch. The animal ran over to greet Kevin, and then turned to stare at Terric, his expression wary. He understood the wolf in Terric, and carefully took its measure. The demon side of him had the dog backing up slightly, until Kevin laid a hand on its back and spoke softly. Terric approached, silently communicating with the animal until it visibly relaxed. Kevin told him its name was Gypsy and he was a rescue. Eventually, Gypsy decided that either Terric wasn't a threat or that he wasn't going to receive any food by hanging around, so he returned to his couch to lay down.

They had brought their plates up and set them in the sink, and then grabbed another beer before heading outside. Kevin's house had a wide front porch, and his part of town was quiet. The night was clear and the sky devoid of extraneous lights. Gypsy followed them out and then took off, bounding across the fenced area. A couple horses wandered around out there and he barked at them, happy to be running free. Terric watched him, envy evident on his face. Kevin noticed, and spoke quietly. "We can join him, if you like. Or you can go by yourself, if you prefer."

Terric shook his head. He wouldn't shift while Kevin stayed in human form. He wasn't that trusting, not yet. And to run together like that, shifting at the same time, too awkward. He was trying to be relaxed about sitting there with Kevin, but he needed to take things slowly for the moment. It wasn't who he normally was. Usually if he had an urge, he gave in to it. Things were too fresh though, with Jordyn. And he wasn't sure he was ready to explore whatever the hell this was with Kevin. "No, not tonight. I'm good, but thanks."

He drank deeply from his beer, exhaling as he moved his head back and forth, cracking his neck. His eyes were serious as he turned to Kevin. "I don't know about any of this, you know? I've been with Jordy for a long time. Before her, there was a human woman. Michelle. That was doomed from the start, but damn, she was interesting." He broke off, the image of Michelle's pretty face in his mind for a moment before he turned back to Kevin.

Kevin chuckled lightly, leaning forward and sitting with his elbows resting on his knees, the beer held loosely in his left hand. "Terric, stop, okay? I didn't ask you here so I could coerce you into anything you aren't ready for. I can't read people, not like you can. But I can tell you're interested. And that you don't know what to do with that interest yet. You don't need to know right now. I just wonder, are you closed off to exploring that side of you, the one that's interested in me? I can be patient. Hell, I think you need a friend now more than you need anything more complicated." He sat back, letting his words sink in.

Terric seemed like one of those insanely independent types, and frankly, it had surprised Kevin to learn that Terric had lived with someone. His eyes traveled over Terric's body, appreciating the way his shirt stretched across his shoulders and the strength evident in the lean frame. Terric didn't appear to be against homosexuality, so that couldn't have been the issue. He didn't have the homophobia bullshit going on. Curiosity got the best of him finally, and he asked the question that had been circling his head for some time. "Did you ever have a relationship with another man, of any type? I mean, even one that was strictly sexual… Did you mess around with someone and it wasn't your thing?"

Terric gave a sardonic laugh, draining his beer and holding up the empty. "I'm going to grab another. You ready for one?" Kevin nodded at him, anxious for an answer but willing to give Terric some space for the moment, clearly the reason he was getting up at that moment. When Terric returned, he set Kevin's beer on the little table between them, and then sat down, opening his own and drinking deeply, as if fortifying himself.

He had a light buzz going on, not nearly enough to make this conversation easy. Nothing would, so best to just get it over with. He stared straight ahead, not meeting Kevin's eyes as he spoke, his voice a monotone. "No. I've never been in a relationship with a man. Male. Whatever. I've always dated women. But I knew, for as long as I can remember, that I was interested in both genders, mostly males. I just haven't acted on it. Willingly." He sensed Kevin grow more still, and flicked his glance over at him, shaking his head slightly to ward off questions or comments.

When he had Kevin's nod, he looked back out into the distance, continuing. "My father was a demon, as I said. Quite a high ranking one. There's a social order, even there. I won't ever be that high up, I'm hybrid, and that means weaker than full demon. It doesn't bother me, I would prefer to be just a shifter and have none of the other bullshit. Well, let me rephrase. If I have to be a demon, I would rather not be weaker than the others, but I've grown used to that. And it doesn't really change the way of things, in the other realm. There, no one is immune to the depravity that goes on. Our existence is at the whim of the demon master, who answers directly and only to Satan. We are often summoned, for various reasons. And there are times that we are called to task, for any reason, or no reason. A big part of it is to bring us to heel. Force us to submit, in acknowledgment of our place. It's not always physical, and truly, most of the time even when it is, it's not really happening. The images, the sensations, it's all there. The pain, the humiliation. None of it is any less real, or less vivid, simply because it's only going on in your head. Does that make sense? You can't tell the difference between whether it's really happening and whether you are being fed the hallucination. Both have happened and I've never really been able to differentiate.

"There is no free will, no private thoughts. And it's just as bad when you are the one who has been chosen to help torture another demon. There is a constant battle among us, down there, to better our stations, and gain favor among the master and the higher demons. I don't know why, really; it's fleeting at best. But down there, it can't be helped, that urge to rise above those around you. It's like a compulsion, which makes sense. We all have that ability; so of course, it's being used against us there. The wolf suffers. That's the worst part for me. Feeling the two parts of me torn, and knowing that the only part of me that has any redeeming qualities dies a little each time I am summoned."

Terric glanced at Kevin once more. His head tilted, and he stared into Kevin's intense blue eyes for a moment. "That's not what you asked, was it? I veered off topic." He turned away again, needing the distance from that compassionate gaze. "Yes. I've had sex with men before, in that context. I don't know if I could do it in any normal way, or if I would lose it, you know? I'm not me when I'm there. I can't be. I don't get summoned often, hardly ever, actually. I'm good at what I do, and the ones above me know what it costs me to be there. I've some friends, if you can call them that. They look out for me. Everything there is about gaining favor."

He closed his mouth, unsure what else was left to say. Kevin set his beer down and moved to crouch beside Terric's chair. His eyes were kind, and he waited silently for Terric to look down at him. His voice was soft, patient. "No, Terric. That... I don't want to say that it doesn't count. It does. But not in the right way, you know? I'm sorry. So fucking sorry-"

Terric stood angrily, his face closed off, mask firmly in place. "Don't fucking do that. Ever. Don't you ever feel sorry for me. Demons exist. Should I wish it on someone else then? Besides, demons are essential. Every being is, but yes, demons are necessary. Balance, Kevin. Without balance, nothing survives. In a perfect world, evil wouldn't exist. But it does. And we come to collect that evil, take it where mortals and immortals alike are apart from it. Separate. Safe. Angels protect. We do as well, just in a different way. I'm not less, because I'm demon."

Terric thrust his hand angrily through his hair, nearly tearing it out of his head. "Hell, maybe I am. *Fuck!* I don't have the words." He looked at Kevin once more, some of the anger gone. "I don't know if I have a soul or not. I would say no, but the wolf... I don't know." He exhaled, shaking his head slightly. "Sounds like something you want to sign on for, doesn't it? Did it work? Did I drive you away yet?"

Kevin stood up, stepped in close to Terric and stared into his eyes. His wolf did the same, appraising the hybrid before him. Something apparently agreed with the wolf, because Kevin felt a shot of pure lust hit him in the gut. His hand reached up, and he ignored the fact that Terric pulled his head back slightly. He placed his palm against Terric's neck and felt Terric swallow nervously. His voice was level, and he spoke simply. "You have a soul, Terric. Don't ever doubt that. It's there. I can see it. I'm going to kiss you, because my wolf is dying for a taste, and honestly, I am, too. I can bet you've never been kissed before, down there in the other realm. And I want to be the first man to kiss you. Tonight. Now."

Kevin didn't wait for Terric to nod or give permission. Neither of them were that type. He moved closer, their chests almost touching. They were nearly the exact same height. Kevin's face was mere inches from Terric's. He could hear Terric's heart pounding, and he smiled darkly, glad to be the one causing that reaction. He wanted to see what else he could make Terric's body do, but that would have to wait. His lips were centimeters from Terric's, and he inhaled deeply, learning his scent. Terric was scarcely breathing, and Kevin knew the demon had considered shoving him away more than once, perhaps kicking his ass. It didn't matter. He needed a taste, and he knew Terric needed this as well. His lips kissed Terric's softly, tentatively at first. It was less of a kiss, more the barest of touches. It wasn't enough.

His wolf was growing restless. Wanting more. His tongue lightly touched the seam of Terric's lips. He licked lightly, making it clear what he wanted. Terric's mouth opened, and he immediately deepened the kiss. His tongue delved into Terric's mouth, stroking over every surface. The kiss was all he knew it would be…The need for that little taste he had been after grew to an urgency, and he wanted more still. He growled low, pulling Terric closer to him.

Terric's thoughts were scattered. He was cataloging his

reaction to Kevin's nearness. Deciding how he felt about it, how comfortable he was with the situation, struggling to maintain control if the situation became dangerous. His wolf was straining, fighting him, unused to being restrained or letting anyone else take control. It pushed relentlessly, insisting he take over the kiss, reclaim his alpha status. Terric returned the kiss while fighting back the wolf. His body was reacting, rapidly growing hard and wanting more.

He indulged himself, letting some of his control slip. His hands moved over Kevin's body, learning the feel of him, surprised that he enjoyed the sensation of another man's body pressed against his. As he let his control slip, his senses spread out, and he moved in, reading Kevin without intending to. He was stunned by the magnitude of Kevin's arousal, the urgency behind it. The shifter wanted to take him, but was holding back. Barely.

Terric's wolf snarled, pushing harder, and the urge to dominate nearly overwhelmed Terric. He shoved Kevin, hard, into the side of the house, using his body to pin him there. He felt Kevin's lust and he began to move, causing enough friction to drive them both crazy. The breath rushed out of him, and he knew his eyes had turned and that the demon was winning.

He forced himself to pull back before he took what wasn't his to take, and what he likely wasn't ready for. He stood there, shaken. They both were breathing hard, and he wanted nothing more than to take Kevin and get back to where they were a few minutes prior. He couldn't, though. It had to be him doing it, for the right reasons, not the evil inside him taking for the sake of taking.

"I have to go. I'm sorry, but I can't be here right now.

Thanks for dinner." He turned, dug his truck keys out of his pocket and stared at them for a moment. It had been long enough; he was fine to drive. It had almost been tempting to leave the truck, using the beers as an excuse to sober up and come back later. Except he was sober as a judge and he needed distance. He didn't know if he would be back, either.

He had to decide it was worth the risk, to either of them. The engine turned over on the first try, and he pulled forward. It took him directly in front of Kevin and he waved as he passed, his eyes never once leaving the road to meet the shifter's stare.

Kevin stood there, his cock aching as need pounded through him. It had gone further than he intended, much further. He had his answer though. Terric wasn't ready, but he wasn't unaffected or uninterested. Kevin smiled to himself, pleased to have pulled that much information out of the taciturn demon. He called out to Gypsy as he picked up the beer bottles, then turned and opened the door, letting them both inside and carrying the stuff to the kitchen as the wooden screen door banged shut.

Chapter Eleven

TERRIC HAD TAKEN to walking the beach just about every day, no matter the weather. He used the time to let his mind rest, and so that he could be alone without the walls of his apartment staring back at him accusingly. He spent too many hours sitting there, replaying different stages in his life. His mind started acting like one of those children's pick-a-path books. He would go back to the moment of decision, when he was at a crossroads, and try to change his path, play out the course of events on the choice he didn't make. A fruitless, and frustrating exercise. He hadn't the means to change the events that had brought him to where he now stood. When he grew tired of berating himself for the way he had lived his life, he then began to recall all the beings he had killed, all the souls he had taken. Each had taken its toll, taking a little piece of who he was and changing it. He felt soiled, deep into the core of his being.

Not one specific instance that had brought him to this point. Nothing he could point to that had been the precipitating factor in the storm that was brewing inside him. The storm was there, though, and demanded he not ignore it. To do so would virtually guarantee that he would spiral out of control, taking out not just any evil around him, but likely many innocent lives as well. That was one of the reasons he had avoided Kevin, and for once, not simply a convenient excuse. He had spoken to Lucas, knowing he owed the other demon an explanation, a warning. Lucas had nodded in understanding, and had taken to swapping roles with Terric for the time being. Lucas worked Ascendance, while Terric dealt with the worst of the lowlife that Trespass did business with, and avoided everyone else.

HE HAD LEFT work in the middle of the night with a thunderstorm moving in. The air was charged with electricity, and the clouds were moving quickly across the sky, allowing periodic glimpses of the moon. When he pulled into the parking lot, he stared at the lighthouse for a long while before getting out of his truck. No one was around, which was what he had been counting on.

Terric walked across the boardwalk and down the few steps to the beach. Whitecaps topped the waves, and he could hear them crashing against the rocks. The tide was coming in, and the wind was picking up. He couldn't see any boats out to sea, and that was a good thing. The beacon made its continuous sweep, and he turned to stare at the lighthouse. He sensed no movement, and he figured the keeper, Adam, was asleep for the night.

Lightning cut across the sky, illuminating the surf and Terric inhaled, breathing in the scents of the storm and the ocean. The hairs on his arm and the back of his neck stood on end. The storm was as close as it could be. His heart pounded, adrenaline pumping through him and he turned his head up to the sky, feeling the cold rain pelt his face.

Terric smiled, his eyes blinking to clear the water from them and then he continued toward the surf. He kept going, closer, the churning of the water calling him, drawing him toward its black depths. He wanted to be in the water, to swim as he remembered Jordyn swimming. He knew he wouldn't appear as she always did, but maybe he could capture that feeling she always seemed to derive from it. When she swam, she was always so fucking free. There was nothing holding her, weighing her or anchoring her.

He himself had always thought he needed that, to be anchored, but maybe that was his problem all along. The water was just above his ankles when another strike of lightning rent the air. It forked into hundreds of jagged lines, spreading out and seeking something to destroy. His stare was locked on it, and he moved farther into the ocean. His knees were wet now, and he watched still, waiting for the thunder that would soon follow. When it did, the sound was deafening and he yelled into it, shouting as loud as he could. The wind took his cry and the thunder obscured it, leaving his ears ringing with the emptiness that met him.

He progressed farther, the water at his waist, tears streaming from his eyes to mingle with the rain. He let his hands submerge, drawing the water up and bringing it to his face, splashing himself so that he couldn't tell the difference between the salt from the ocean and the salt from his tears. His head fell backward as the lightning struck again, is if he were imploring it to find him. His wolf was silent, as Terric debated, edging farther away from the beach and the lighthouse and safety.

The beacon passed over him once more. He hadn't even noticed its last several passes. He realized then how far he had disappeared into his own head. A hand gripped his upper arm just then, and he whirled around, eyes bleeding instantly to red. He wasn't caught unaware, ever. He didn't raise a hand to protect himself, however. And when he saw who it was, he felt relief that he hadn't.

Adam stood silently, his eyes solemn. He didn't speak. It would have been pointless to. No one could hear anything above the storm. Terric's eyes moved up and down, as if seeing the man for the first time. Adam appeared anywhere between fifty and sixty, when in truth, he was easily twice that. He was human, for the most part. Immortal human, and just as trapped as Terric was. He gestured for Terric to follow him, and for some reason, the demon did as he was bid. They made their way back to the beach, Terric's stride shorter to accommodate Adam's slower pace. The human was drenched; having followed Terric into the surf when shouting had proved fruitless.

They both turned at the same time, hearing the lightning rend the air and then the boom of thunder. The sky still illuminated enough that they didn't need the arc of light from the beacon to show them the waterspout that hit not twenty yards from where they stood. Adam flicked his glance at Terric for a moment, and then they both turned and continued walking.

AT THE ENTRANCE to Adam's house, they stopped, and clumsily pulled off sodden shoes and socks. Adam grabbed a couple towels from a mudroom just inside the front door. He handed Terric one and then started to dry himself as well, leading him deeper into his home to a winding staircase and when T started to hesitate, gruffly told him to follow. They entered Adam's sparse bedroom, and Adam opened a couple drawers, pulling out two pairs of sweat pants and a couple long sleeve shirts. He opened another drawer, grabbed a large pair of cotton socks, and handed the pile to Terric. When Terric stood there holding the items, Adam gestured to a bathroom across the hall and told him to shower if he wanted to, then head down to the living room when he was ready.

The bathroom was neat, empty of all but the essentials. Terric laid the clothes on the counter and removed his wet garments. He stood before the mirror for a moment, ignoring the cold, and just stared at himself. The fire brand was there, as always. It held no heat at the moment. It simply looked like an amazingly real tattoo. It was over his heart, and when one stared at it long enough, they could swear the flame was alive and they saw it move and twist as a real flame would. The movement was an illusion, but the fire served as a warning, a hint to others of what the one who bore it was. He saw that his eyes appeared dead, his face drawn.

Demons sometimes fell into a coma-like rest, deep enough to allow mind and body to heal. It happened often upon returning from the other realm, but it hadn't happened to him in awhile, and he was glad. He would head there soon, however, if he weren't careful. He turned toward the shower, pulled back the curtain and turned on the water, waiting for the older pipes to kick in and do their thing. Finally, the water began to come from the showerhead and he stepped in under the spray, turning it as hot as it could go and letting it warm his body.

He let the water wash the salt from his skin and hair, and

he felt exhaustion hit him. He stood there for several minutes and then shut the water off. He was wrapping the towel around his hips as he stepped out, and from somewhere else in the house he heard another shower turn off, and he was glad the lighthouse had two bathrooms; he hadn't made Adam wait for him to finish.

After he dressed, he did as instructed and headed downstairs to the main living areas. Several photographs were scattered around, mostly on the walls, as there weren't many places with horizontal surfaces. Adam seemed to dislike having a lot of stuff, and Terric could appreciate that. Several black and white photos were of one woman. She was lovely, appearing to be in her early twenties. He saw many photos of her and a younger looking Adam, and as Terric walked along the wall and checked out more photographs, he saw old-fashioned looking pictures of Adam with what must have been his family growing up. They looked happy, all of them.

Terric thought for a moment, on the way of family. The closeness in the beginning and then, as the children grow, the way the dynamics change. Human families were far more complex than immortals; he had learned that long ago. The humans dealt with things an immortal wouldn't often have to face. Death, loss, the way people grew apart because they were hampered by time and distance, and the relentless necessity of building a life while earning a living.

There were photos of Adam as a child with children that were clearly siblings of his. And family shots, all of them crowded together, obviously stiff and posed. One was taken in front of the lighthouse they stood in now, and Terric noted that it still looked much the same as it had back then. All of the more recent photos were of animals. Many different dogs, some in pairs and some alone, as well as several different cats. He peered at each, studying them with the same interest as he had shown in the human photos. And he learned something more about Adam at that moment. He had spent the past several decades alone, animals being his only friends and companions. Terric felt Adam watching him, and he turned and watched the human, the one human who could stand in a room with him and feel no fear.

Terric spoke softly, his tone matter of fact but not without compassion. "You've been alone for so long."

Adam gestured to the photos. "Not alone. I have my animals. They're my friends. Animals have always been my friends, even when I had human contact and friendship. Companionship. Love." He turned to head to the kitchen.

Terric followed, deliberately shutting down the part of his mind that wanted to dig into Adam's brain and just find the memories and view them for himself. "Yes. I can understand that. But you aren't like us. You're not a shifter. You can't really communicate with them."

Adam turned to Terric, annoyance showing on his face. "Yes. I can. I may not be able to talk their language or they mine, but we understand each other just fine. Too many people don't know how to be quiet and just listen. Animals do that instinctively. They know what I am saying, and I know what they are telling me. Do you think you need to be an animal to be a friend to them?"

TERRIC SPOKE QUIETLY, and with respect. "No. I don't think that. But most humans do."

ADAM RETURNED TO what he was doing. He filled a pot with

water and set about making coffee. Without turning, he gestured to the refrigerator and told Terric where to find the sandwich fixings Terric's eyebrows shot up in surprise, unable to quite believe that Adam, a human, had basically just ordered the demon to make him a sandwich. When he didn't hear movement, Adam turned to frown at Terric when he finally spoke. "They aren't going to make themselves, and I'm hungry. It's not every day I have to haul myself into a storm and drag some demon out of harm's way." His expression didn't change, but he winked, and Terric could see the grin as Adam turned to fill the coffee filter with grounds.

THE SMELL OF coffee began to fill the small kitchen just as Terric was putting the top slice of bread onto each sandwich. He had kept it simple; ham and cheese with mustard and mayo, and he had sliced up a tomato he found. He used a slice on each sandwich and then sliced the rest and divided it between the two plates. He set one down in front of Adam at the table, and his own beside it before heading over to pour the coffee into the waiting mugs.

Terric turned to Adam and raised a brow, to which Adam shook his head. T grabbed a couple paper towels and headed back to the table with the mugs of black coffee. They sat and ate in comfortable silence for several minutes. The bread was homemade and the coffee strong, and both warmed him. He hadn't had homemade anything in months, and he hadn't realized he missed it.

Terric spoke first. "How long have you been alone, human?" He knew the basics behind Adam's story, and Adam wasn't the first human who had been changed. This was different though. He hadn't been altered so that some immortal being could claim him as servant or pet. He had been changed and then left without explanation. Adam's change was crueler, actually. At least the other way, he would have had some sort of contact with other people, and a reason for what had been done.

ADAM'S VOICE WAS thoughtful. "A long time. A hundred years, maybe? No, it just seems like that, I guess. I had to leave my family, once it became obvious. I am aging, but so slowly. I was twenty seven at the turn of the last century. I was courting a girl, and I had family and friends. I stayed in that life for as long as I could. Hell, at first, I didn't even know anything was different. My girl and I married, and we made a life. We weren't blessed with children." His face closed off for a moment, and Terric knew that was a subject that wouldn't be revisited between the two. Adam continued. "My wife knew that something was wrong. Probably before I did. And then it made sense what the otherworlder had said to me that night. We moved away from everyone and kept in touch through letters, and then phone calls. She would go visit her people once every couple of years, and stop in and see mine as well. She would bring me back photos and stories. And she would make my excuses to everyone; say I was sick or that I was working, or stationed out of the country. Back in those days, it was harder to visit, so they believed her. They thought I was lost at sea, eventually. She hated that, telling them that lie, but they were all growing old. Grandkids had been born, and I knew none of them any longer. My parents died, and then my siblings. They never gave up searching for me. Thinking back, it would have been kinder to tell them I was dead. We always hoped, though, that something would happen. A miracle, and whatever had been done to me would stop, and I could continue on with the progression of a normal human life. My wife died coming home from my sister's funeral. I wanted nothing more than to die with her, to be buried beside her."

Adam drank more of his coffee. He finished his sandwich and ate a slice of tomato, moving the plate around idly for a minute before continuing. "After awhile, I put away all the photos she brought from those trips. I have boxes filled with the lives of people I never had a chance to know. I kept out the ones of people whose lives I was a part of, even if it weren't for long enough. I always used to complain about not having enough time. And now, I would give anything in the world to have been limited to the same amount of time as those I loved."

Terric listened. His stillness would have unnerved another human, perhaps, but Adam had lived among others like him for decades; he had no reason to pretend. Normally, he didn't ask people questions, knowing what it was like to want privacy. He sensed Adam's need to talk, though, and it matched his own. And it took his mind off his own shit for a while, a welcome reprieve. "What made you come here?"

Adam smiled at a memory and it made Terric, once again, want to sneak inside his head, even to experience the memory secondhand. He refrained, and Adam continued talking. "My grandfather was the lighthouse keeper when I was a kid. It's been in my family for generations, and it's one of the few that are still privately owned and civilian run. I mean, I'm a civilian now. I was in the Navy as a young man, but that's another lifetime ago. It's in my blood, and what I would have wanted to be anyway, so I'm lucky in that regard. I grew up here. My extended family was scattered around Massachusetts; Franklin, Boston, Wrentham, all over, even up to Worcester. But we, my parents and us kids, our grandparents, we always lived here, on the tip of Cape Cod. I remember when the paranormal types started moving in. No one understood what they were. My little sister saw one and was staring at her for the longest time. My mother nervously told her to stop it, that staring was rude. And my sister, as little kids tend to do, blurted out for all to hear. I remember, she said no, that the lady was so beautiful that she had to come from another world. The lady came over and approached my sister, knelt so they were the same level, and playfully pulled one of her long braids. My sister, Linda, was only about four or five at the time. She giggled, and her little hand reached out and touched that lady's face. My mom rushed forward, and so did I. I don't know what we thought we were going to do against such a being. But the beautiful lady simply smiled and stood, raising a hand to tell us it was okay. Her voice was charming and a pleasure to listen to. She must have been able to read minds; she knew our names. And she said 'Don't worry, Adam, Mrs. Johansson, Linda's right.' And then she winked at Linda and left. Linda ran around telling everyone the story of how she had made a new friend, an 'otherworlder'. And the expression stuck, somehow, to this day. We all know you're from this world, but still. It was the first real sign we had that these beings were friends of a sort."

Terric chuckled, glad to hear that there had been kindness shown a child, and that they hadn't run into one of the darker souls that moved among them. He picked up his empty plate, and Adam's, and carried them over to the sink. He finished his coffee before setting it beside the plates and turned to

Adam. "Thank you for sharing your story with me. And now I understand why you call us 'others' or 'otherworlders', it makes sense." He smiled, his face relaxed and his eyes less stressed. It had been good, talking to the lighthouse keeper.

ADAM INTERRUPTED HIM, his voice serious. "You leaving, wolf? Sorry, for some reason, I prefer to think of you as wolf instead of demon. You don't have to go, you know. If you need someplace to hang out for awhile."

Terric shook his head and thanked him once more. He went upstairs and retrieved his wet clothes, holding them under his arm. "I'll wash these things and return them to you. I won't be far, but I think it's best I sleep in my own place tonight. I need to get settled back into my life, and for some reason, I'm not as settled as I thought I was. I'd like to come back though. You know, hang out. Talk. Whatever it is that friends do."

Adam's brow lowered in a mock frown. He wasn't comfortable with words, interactions. He had lived in his memories and silence for a long time. But still, he warmed at the idea. He rose and walked Terric to the heavy front door, opening it and stepping outside. The rain was nearly stopped, and the air smelled clean, no longer dangerous. "Don't be a stranger, then. I'll see you soon."

Chapter Twelve

TERRIC WAS NEARLY at his truck when he stopped dead, immediately aware that something was wrong. He let his senses spread out and he searched the entire area for the threat. Not a threat, precisely, more like something was off, out of place. He tossed his clothes into the bed of his truck as he approached and then stared into the cab. He sighed in annoyance and unlocked the door. The kid's head had been on the armrest and he jerked awake when he felt it ripped away from him.

Devon. Terric stood there, blocking the open door, and folded his arms as he stared at the kid. Devon's eyes were huge in his head and he was about to piss himself. He sat up, staring straight ahead, and then his eyes shifted to the passenger door, as if gauging how far he could make it before he was caught. Terric glared at him, and kept his tone unfriendly when he finally spoke. "Don't even try it, kid. All it's going to do is make me chase you on a full stomach, and that will piss me off. You're caught, so man up. Why the fuck are you in my truck?"

Devon's voice was small at first, and then he recalled Terric's 'man up' comment and he put some force behind it, enough to be heard, at least. "I had nowhere to go. I was here at the beach when the storm moved in, and I couldn't figure out where to go. I saw your truck, so I broke in." He saw the tic in the man's jaw and hurriedly continued. "I'm good at it. I didn't hurt nothing. Besides, this thing is so old…" He broke off again when he thought about what that may have sounded like, and slid his gaze up at the guy and shut his mouth.

Terric's mouth was a grim line. Then he realized what the kid said. The cab driver had assured him that the kid had been brought back to a house. Though nothing fancy, people were living there, a family. "It's a classic, not just an old truck. What the fuck is it lately with people hating on it?" He drew in a breath. And then another. "Okay, kid. You have family, where are they?"

Devon stared at the dashboard as he spoke. At one point, he propped his foot up on it but then wisely pulled it down. Truthfully though, he wasn't really afraid of the guy, although he knew he should be. Something told him that this man wouldn't have any interest in hurting him, or even being particularly mean. He wasn't friendly or anything. He didn't give off warmth but more of a… caring vibe. As if he ended up caring despite himself. And that gave Devon the strength to continue.

He spoke in a monotone, as if relaying someone else's story. "I was kicked out, I guess. Well, my mother was. She was living with some guy, and I live with her. Most of the time, she lets me, and she takes me with her if she leaves. She was pissed that I came home the other day all beat up and that I was broke. Said she would be blamed for it. She ah… She has a bad temper, but normally she doesn't hit much, she just yells and stuff. Anyway, when I came home from school yesterday, I couldn't get in the house. I knocked and the guy, her boyfriend, opened the door. He said she was gone and that I should be too. I asked for my stuff and he laughed. He went to slam the door on me and I blocked him from closing it all the way. He punched me in the face, and then pulled out a gun. I took off running. I don't know where she is. I can't find her anywhere. I don't know where to go." He didn't mention that he had seen the truck at that club, and that he had seen who owned it. "I'm sorry, for breaking in; I just wanted to get out of the storm." He turned and met Terric's eyes for the first time, and tried to scrape together some dignity. "I don't ask for handouts. I just… can I crash in your truck for the rest of the night?"

Terric jerked his head up, motioning for the kid to move over, which he did, making room for Terric to slide behind the wheel. He started the truck and then began driving, trying to think about what to say. "Kid, I'm not going to have you sleeping in my truck. That's just not okay. If you're lying to me, and you're some dumbass runaway, I will find that out real quick. You can stay at my place a couple days, and that's it. We'll try to find your mother and if we can't, then we'll find your father." He caught the quick shake of the kid's head and continued smoothly. "No father, okay. That's not a problem. We'll find your mother. I want to talk to her a bit anyway." He drove on a few miles, just to give the kid time to relax. His hands tightened on the wheel when he thought of some guy pulling a gun on a kid. "Don't worry; I'll pick up your stuff for you. You stay away from there. Is it the same place the cab brought you to the other night?" Devon nodded and T filed away the information, knowing he had some business to attend to the following night. "My name's Terric."

Devon exhaled, his hands still shaky, and he heard his stomach growl. He tightened his stomach muscles and tried to make it stop, which did no good. So he started to talk, trying to distract himself. "You're not human. Right?" Terric ignored his question and pulled into the parking lot of a Taco Bell. He asked what Devon wanted, and Devon shook his head. "Nothing. I don't have any cash." Terric went silent, pulled up to the drive through, and ordered more food than Devon had ever seen anyone get at one time.

TERRIC GRABBED THE bag from the drive through kid and shoved it at Devon as he drove away. "Eat, dammit. I don't want your money, and before you give me any bullshit about not accepting charity, you should have thought of that before you broke into my truck." The kid's hurt feelings emanated across the enclosed space of the cab and Terric felt a pang of remorse. "Listen, kid, we've all needed a hand, you know? So, take the hand that's offered and just remember to extend yours to someone in need someday."

They drove the rest of the way to the apartment in silence. The kid clutched the bag on his lap, and Terric could hear his stomach growling. He got out, and the kid followed suit, locking his door as Terric had, and they started heading to the stairs. T heard the kid trudging tiredly behind him and he slowed his pace, waiting for the kid to catch up. The sky was turning light, and he knew the kid had to be exhausted. He couldn't have gotten more than an hour or two of sleep. He punched in the security code and held the door open for the kid, and they made their way up the stairs. When they were inside, Terric dropped his keys, then remembered his clothes down in the truck. He waved his hand toward the kitchen table and told the kid to start eating. He ran down and grabbed the still soaking items and brought them back up, leaving them on the washing machine before he entered the kitchen. The kid was stuffing his face, and looked like he had already polished off two of the tacos. He didn't really eat like a pig; his manners were sloppy only because he was so hungry. Terric grabbed a bottle of water and sat beside him.

THE KID TRIED to be polite, set down his food and finished chewing before speaking. "How can you go out during the day light?"

Terric pointed to the wrapped food. "Keep eating, kid. I'm not a fucking vampire. That's how." He noticed the kid swallowed hard and he made his tone less surly. "Sorry, kid. Habit. Anyway. Not all paranormals are vampires. I'm hybrid. Demon and wolf-shifter. So, daylight is fine for me. And hell, some vampires can stand it too, if they aren't full vampire. My Jordyn was vampire, and couldn't tolerate a second of it." He realized he was rambling, but truly, he had no idea how to talk to a kid.

He couldn't pretend to be into the small talk bullshit, asking about school and what grade the kid was in. He stared around his place, trying to work out the logistics of where to put the kid. He wasn't ready to have anyone in Jordyn's room, and it didn't seem right to let the kid take his while he took the couch. They had a third room that they used as an office of sorts, but it had no bed. Finally, he got up and grabbed some blankets and a couple pillows from the closet, dumping them on the couch. "You'll be fine there, it's only for one or two nights, remember? I don't normally have guests. I see you finished the food, you want anything else? I know it's not much of a breakfast, but I don't think anything else was open that late. Or early, depending on how you look at it."

"You kidding me? Tacos are my favorite food, doesn't matter what time of day." Devon stood and threw his wrappers away, drained his soda and tossed the cup out. He asked where the bathroom was, and went where Terric pointed. When he came back, he set up a bed on the couch, arranging the pillows and lying down stiffly. He saw Terric watching him and he sat up, resting his chin on his palm. "Thanks for letting me crash here. I won't stay long or be in the way or anything."

TERRIC NODDED AND turned out the kitchen lights, then willed the door to the playroom locked. He turned on a lamp next to the couch and handed the kid the remote. When he was almost out of the room, the kid stopped him with a question. He turned back, his expression thoughtful. "Yeah, kid. We'll find her. One way or another, we will. Now go to sleep. You can stay home from school today, but you have to go back tomorrow."

The kid slept throughout the entire day, which was good. Terric paid the mother's boyfriend a visit. The man was vile. The house stank, and the yard was overgrown, it looked like the place had been deserted for years. It was hard to imagine the kid living like that, or any mother keeping her kid in those conditions. When Terric banged on the door, the man opened it, a snarl on his face as he asked who the fuck was there. Terric held silent, waiting for the man to figure out that what he was staring at wasn't good. He could hear the man's thoughts. He had assumed that Terric was code enforcement back again, and he had grabbed his gun to scare the shit out of the enforcement officer.

That pissed Terric off even more. He was standing there, and kept the gun away. It seemed that the human only pulled it on people he figured he could intimidate. Terric gripped the man by his shirtfront and shoved him back into the house, following closely. He kicked the door shut and then willed it to lock. The man's eyes widened and Terric smelled the strong ammonia stench of urine. An evil grin spread across T's face and he laughed. "That's all it took, huh? A parlor trick and you're already pissing your pants. Not as brave when it's not a kid or some public servant telling you to clean up the shit hole that you call home."

HE PAUSED, GLANCING around the darkened house. The place was in shambles. They had either had a huge party or there had been a large altercation, most of the worthless crap was broken. "Where's the kid's mother? Did she dump him or did you get rid of her? I'm giving you a chance to tell me before I go inside that greasy mind of yours and take the truth."

The human stammered a few times, and then finally spoke. "She's gone. We had a fight and I kicked her out." At Terric's question, he considered lying for a millisecond but then did the smart thing. "Yeah. I hit her, but she hit me first. She's alive though, and fine. She was drunk and told me she was seeing someone else. She was leaving me anyway. Was planning on leaving the kid to be my problem."

Terric's fist shot out, and he punched the guy, first in the gut, and then, when he was doubled over, he landed an uppercut to the jaw. He refrained from breaking anything, although he wanted to. His growl was low, mean. "Show me the kid's room. Where his stuff is."

The guy hobbled down the hall, rubbing his jaw and trying to draw in a deep breath. He pointed wordlessly to a room that was, while not nice by any means, neater than the rest of the house. A large box sat on the floor, open as if waiting to be filled. Terric looked at the guy, curious, and then understood. The guy had been planning on selling Devon's stuff, the only thing in the house that wasn't destroyed. Terric tersely told him to pack it all up, neatly. The human frowned at him as if to argue and then closed his mouth, walked into the room, and began to comply.

Terric leaned against the doorframe and watched, ensuring at the end there was nothing left but the ratty furniture. He opened every drawer and checked into every possible area that a kid could or would hide shit that was important to him. He was doing a final check when he felt the floorboard move beneath his foot. He walked over to the box, grabbed out a pocketknife he had watched get dropped in there, and went over to the loosened floorboard. He dropped to one knee and used the knife to pry it open, and then reached in and pulled out two boxes. One had pictures and folded up notes, and the other was a small, metal lockbox. The thing was locked, and he had no interest as to its contents anyway. It belonged to Devon though, and he was glad he had found it. He set both inside the box the human had packed and started heading toward the door. He instructed the human to follow and bring the box out with him.

Once outside, he gestured to the bed of his truck and watched while the box was set down and the tailgate shut. He reached into the glove box of his truck and grabbed pen and paper. And then he spoke one final time. "Stay away from the kid. Completely away. I find out you bothered him and you're done. You see his mother, you send her to Ascendance, tell her to ask for Terric. Here's my number, if she calls, pass it along."

Terric hopped in the truck and turned the key, not sparing the human a glance as he pulled forward, and the guy had to stumble back out of the way. He drove home, carrying the box of stuff up and setting in the office. He drew a couple twenties out of his wallet and laid them on the counter, then wrote a note for Devon, telling him where to find his things, and that he was going to work, to order a pizza and stay inside. It wasn't a request, and he knew Devon would know he was serious, and not set foot out of the apartment.

Terric showered and got ready to go. He checked his phone, judging how early he was going to be and trying to figure out what he wanted to do. Finally, he headed out of his apartment, needing to be alone for the call he was about to make.

THE PHONE RANG several times before it was picked up and he spoke quickly, not wanting to deal with the pretense of polite chatter. "Kevin. Can you meet me at Mulligan's? We need to talk."

Epilogue

THAT FIRST CALL had been the hardest, by far. Terric had arrived at Mulligan's first, and his nerves had been high as he sat nursing a beer. Kevin hadn't asked what he wanted or why Terric wanted to meet up. That would have made things easier, in a way. It would have irritated Terric, someone questioning why he wanted to talk to them. It sounded arrogant, but that was who he was. By the same token, however, he wouldn't question anyone who mattered to him either. His first response would have been assent, and then he would find out the particulars in time. That Kevin merely agreed to show up told Terric he mattered, and that raised the stakes just a bit higher. He wasn't sure he was ready to mean something to someone just yet. Still, he hadn't called to cancel, had merely phoned the club and said he would be in late.

Kevin stopped by the bar and ordered a beer, carrying it over to the table himself so he and T wouldn't be disturbed. His eyes were intent as he stared at the demon, watching the indecision flit across the normally confident features as russet colored eyes were lifted to meet his. He sat down, inhaling deeply as he did. Terric's scent had the same effect on him as it had at every meeting, and his nostrils flared slightly as if to take in more of it.

He waited silently, debating what to say. Finally, he leaned back in his chair, trying to give Terric some room and using his usual easygoing demeanor to lighten the mood. "Looks like you have a lot on your mind, T. You sure you want to do this now? We have plenty of options here. We can let it go, for now. We can wait until you're more settled or we can take this back to your place and just let things progress where we both want them to go. Hell, I change my mind; take back what I said before. You can even use me to experiment on." His charming grin was disarming, and Terric shook his head.

"Ass. Jesus, you really are an ass, you know that? Besides, I can't. It seems I have a roommate for a while." He filled Kevin in on Devon's situation, noting the compassion that Kevin felt for a kid he had never met. For some reason, Terric liked that. A lot. He found himself relaxing, and as he finished his beer, he motioned the waitress over and asked for a couple of menus. They both ordered, and the talk turned to safe, easy topics. Terric had trained himself to block other people's thoughts over the years, so much so he did it automatically. Not with Kevin though, he kept finding himself wanting to explore every facet of who Kevin was, and what he was thinking. It was distracting, but he was enjoying the slow process of coming to know someone, and that helped.

They sat there for a couple of hours, until Terric motioned for the check and waved away Kevin's offer to pay it. "No, I asked you, remember. Besides. Doesn't this count as a date?"

He smirked and set his card down on top of the tab, watching Kevin's face as the waitress headed off with it.

Kevin smiled slightly. "Sure, yeah. I guess. I prefer something a little fancier. I mean, it won't compare to Sloppy Joes and Gypsy begging, but you know. At least try." He leaned forward a bit, his expression growing a bit more serious. "There's no hurry, but I'm glad you called. I enjoy being with you, even just like this."

TERRIC STARED AT him for a moment, weighing his words. "How can you do that, say things like that so easily? I can't, you know. Talk like that, not really. Even with Jordyn, I never really had the words, especially when she really needed them. Or when I needed to say them." He glanced up as the waitress returned with the slip for him to sign. He signed and handed it back to her with a brief nod, his attention still focused on Kevin.

Kevin's face was serious, but kind. "Does it cost anything to say them if you feel them? I guess you have to decide if the person you're saying them to is worth taking a chance on, showing a weakness to. Although how saying something that is true and nice to hear as well as say can be considered a weakness is something I can't understand. We've had different life experiences. Maybe you won't trust as easily as I do. And maybe some things don't need to be said. I know you're enjoying me as well. You don't have to say it. When you're ready, I have a feeling you will find all the words you need. It may never be easy for you to say them, but that will just make them mean more."

Kevin picked up his beer and drained it, then asked Terric if he was ready. Terric nodded, standing and moving his chair back in. The two walked out the door, and Kevin inclined his head at Terric, flashing his trademark half-smile as he winked. "Talk to you soon, T."

The night at work passed uneventfully. When he arrived home, Devon was watching TV, his pose classically bored teenager as he flipped through the channels. Terric asked him if he had eaten, and Devon nodded toward the empty pizza box. Terric sighed, realizing the kid had eaten pizza for dinner and then breakfast, and the only other thing had been tacos. "Kid. I'm not all that much of a nurturer, but we have to buy you some decent food. We can shop later. Can you cook?" Devon shrugged, mumbled a reply that sounded like an affirmative, and Terric lost his patience. Devon still hadn't made eye contact.

T glanced at the TV and willed it off. Devon frowned down at the remote in his hand, and then quickly at Terric, his face lighting up when he realized what had happened. Terric glared at him and shook his head. "Don't even think about it kid. I don't do tricks for people." He had almost tacked on "especially humans" but really, it didn't matter who it was. Besides, this kid was getting on his nerves.

TERRIC TRIED A different track. "School. Don't you need to go?" Devon nodded, and said he would go the following day. Terric headed into Jordyn's room, staring around for a moment, unsure of what he was about to do. The room was basically empty, except in his mind he could still see her stuff, picture her moving gracefully around as she gently smiled at him, talking in a husky voice as she asked about his day. He took a deep breath and shoved the memories aside, vaguely aware that it had hurt less than the last time he had entered the room. He left the door open and called to Devon, and at the questioning gaze, he simply said, "You can move your stuff in here, in case it takes a little longer to find your mother."

Devon sat on the bed and looked around, and Terric could see that there were a million questions buzzing around the kid's head. This room was the lesser of two evils, however. The playroom was packed up but the stuff was sitting there in boxes, waiting to be hauled out to the complex's communal dumpster. Teen boys were teen boys, and human was no different than paranormal when it came to getting into shit they had no business in. He'd move the stuff out the next time he was home and the kid was in school. Terric got up and left the room, giving Devon privacy and space to unpack.

NEARLY A WEEK passed before Terric was able to catch some down time. He and Devon had actually started to settle in to a routine of sorts, and the kid was losing the tentative air he had, revealing his true smartass nature. When the kid overcame his fear of T, his mouth took over and it was clear that when he felt safe, his intelligence and wit drove him to push on without a filter or any thought of moderating what he said. Terric found himself amused more than he was homicidal, which was good for both he and the kid. He hadn't found the mother, but from random inquiries and some careful questioning of Devon, Terric was just as glad that he hadn't, for the moment. The human woman was, by all accounts, an abusive and bitter drunk. The situation with Devon staying with him wasn't ideal and was by no means permanent, but Terric wanted him to have a chance to breathe for a little while before they decided what came next.

HOWEVER, IT WAS awkward, that first time he told Dev he was going out. Devon had glanced at him, and understanding dawned on his face. He had wondered who the gruff demon dated, and had been dying to ask questions. When he saw that T actually appeared nervous, he had smirked, his cocky grin earning him a narrowed eyed glare. "Who is she? Do I get meet her?"

TERRIC STARED THE kid dead in the eye, and answered without hesitating. "His name's Kevin. And no. You don't." He grabbed his keys and headed toward the door, glad to have the last word for a change. "Behave, punk ass."

www.ingramcontent.com/pod-product-compliance
Lightning Source LLC
Chambersburg PA
CBHW032006170626
46807CB00006B/2682